WOLF:

BOOK 3

"Inferno."

By: A.G. Milhorn

Edited by: Dozer Yukon

Contents

CHAPTER 1

Rakinos stalked the hallways of the underground complex, his heavy foot falls echoing silently in the concrete tunnels. He held the cracked tablet with its screen flickering in his left hand, and for the first time in years, had been stunned into wordlessness. At first, when he first saw the results, he had felt a white-hot rush of anger-- rage so deep that it burned his blood-- but that faded not long after the wheels in his mind began to turn. Most of the rooms were empty since he rarely allowed prisoners to be taken; in all his time as the leader of Lupine Freedom, it was not his policy to leave survivors, especially if they interfered in his plans.

The fact that no one knew that he was the leader of Lupine Freedom and in fact was not simply a disgraced genetics expert pleased him greatly. Of course, in due time, he would reveal himself and take the fight for the supremacy of his kind to the humans directly but for now, this revelation had thrown a significant monkey wrench into his plans and he didn't like it one bit. It was distracting. It was emotional. It was...annoying, he thought as he passed the only room that was currently occupied.

He heard noises behind the thick steel, scrabbling sounds and the long low moan of despair that was stuck somewhere between human and canine misery. Low whimpers and whines echoed in the room and then as he drew near, the sounds suddenly stopped.

Rakinos paused, knowing what was going to happen and waited for the inevitable, his scarlet eyes watching the door almost patiently.

Behind the door there was a heavy scuffling sound as if something or someone had gotten to their feet quickly and was now approaching the door. Something heavy flopped against the steel a moment later, vibrating it silently and two yellow eyes appeared at the top of the door where a small window had been made out of steel mesh. The eyes were reddened around the whites; desperate, afraid, pupils wide and wet. When it spoke, its voice was weak, shaking and pleading, almost mewling. Despite this, it was a familiar voice, one that Rakinos had endured for far too long.

"Please....kill me...let me die...."

Something inside of Rakinos ticked. He hated mewling. He didn't even turn to face the door and said nothing as he began to walk away.

"No... please. Don't go. END THIS!! You betrayed me!!" The voice screamed, its voice going into a high-pitched yelp of desperation.

Rakinos felt his temper flare and reared back his right hand, balling up his fist as he did. He knew the thing's face would be pressed directly up against the metal and struck there, his blow landing hard against the steel, hard enough dent it.

The sound of flesh and bone striking the steel reverberated through the halls.

There was a horrible sound, pitiful in its pathetic whimpers as the blow resonated through the steel and struck the occupants sensitive face. The whimpers became a scream of pure canine agony, a high-pitched canine scream and the eyes shot away from the mesh. Rakinos heard it scuffle to the back of the room and moments later, heard the sound of sniffles and whimpers resume.

Better, he thought.

A guard up the hall glanced towards him and Rakinos didn't have to say a word as the guard wisely looked the other way.

With a low growl, Rakinos made his way up the hall and finally settled in his office, the door hissing shut behind him, sealing him off mercifully from fools and the weak. He tossed the crushed tablet into the corner absently.

Pushing up the arms on his black wooly, he opened a small cabinet and pulled down a heavy glass tumbler. He grabbed a few ice cubes from the mini-fridge on the far table and lastly grabbed a large bottle full of amber liquid with a black label on its side. As he sat at his desk he pondered the label.

Riley's Black Label.

It was one of the few alcohols made strong enough so that a shifter's metabolism wouldn't just give them a light buzz but rather allowed them to actually feel the full effects of the spirit in question.

It was a derivative of bourbon, and it was something to make the pathetic and more well-known Kentucky clans jealous. *Of course,* he thought, *it's not Draco Riley that made the spirit but rather, his little brother, Ash.*

He poured a tumbler full and let his mind drift to the younger Riley. Ash owned the Wolves Den club and was noticeably less amicable towards politics of any sort. That sort of neutral environment made it easy for people like Rakinos to take advantage of it as an information tap, and he had been using the club as a way to get intel and keep his ears on the cultural and political scene in the shifter community. Keeping his head down and staying quiet, so far, it had served him well. Once he revealed himself fully, however, if his plans came to fruition, he knew that connection would be cut off as cleanly as a limb with a laser scalpel.

Ash may not be one for the politics but he won't tolerate the truth once he becomes aware that I'm using his club and the people in it for my own ends, Rakinos thought, taking a slow drink.

Ash had cornered him on his first night there after he caught Rakinos entering the club. Rakinos remembered it even now, years later.

Ash had been behind the bar talking to his barkeep when he caught sight of Rakinos entering past security. Ash had immediately stormed out from behind the bar and charged across the dining room, grabbed Rakinos by the forearm and pulled him aside.

"What the hell are you doing here?" the younger Riley had snarled.

Rakinos had given him a cold smile.

"I'm here to relax, like everyone else."

Riley snarled, barely keeping his voice low.

"What the fuck do you think you're doing here you red furred bastard? Give me one reason to not throw you out in the streets with the rest of the shit! Or better," Ash growled, *baring his fangs. "Give me a reason not to break your fucking face."*

Rakinos raised his eyebrows. "Do you still think I had a hand in your sister's death? Why would I? She was one of us, even as human as she was."

Ash's silver and black furred face was a storm of rage as Rakinos lowered his large red-furred head and his eyes gleamed. His voice was low and rough.

"I didn't kill your sister and I had nothing to do with her death. A human man killed her, the same ones your brother wants to make peace with. I made sure he never made it home. Now, can I get a drink in peace or are you going to be like your big brother and let polit-

ics and the past dictate your life? Or will you be your own man?"

Ash seemed to consider the words and slowly, reluctantly, let the bigger werewolf go.

"Just don't drag your shit in here. I don't want any of it. No politics. This is a safe space for people like us."

Rakinos remembered straightening his shirt and as Ash had walked away, he called out:

"Are you going to tell your brother?"

Ash paused and looked over his shoulder. "It's my business. My club. I control who I let in and out but I can't ban you without a reason. I don't answer to my brother either. But I swear, the moment you stick one toe across the line, you're out."

Rakinos smiled. Ash was easy to work over. He sensed the strain between the brothers, given their lack of public appearances together and suspected that Ash, like all young brothers, suffered from living in his brother's shadow and so had applied just the right pressure and secured himself nicely in the club without further incident.

In fact, he relished the thought seeing the look on Draco's face when the truth came out. Draco had spent every waking moment of the last few decades combating what the old man considered Lupine Freedom's message of violence and resistance, of werewolf superiority.

It would be glorious to finally reveal to both Rileys that both of them had been duped and used like pawns in a long game by the leader of Lupine Freedom itself. Rakinos allowed himself a small knowing smile as he poured the tumbler full of amber liquid, the ice floating to the top with a gentle clink.

The sharp anti-septic scent of the alcohol wafted up into his nose and he raised his glass, closing his eyes as he inhaled it, letting the smell warm up his taste buds as it flowed through him. When he finally took the drink, the liquid seemed to jitter and dance in his mouth like it was alive, bouncing swirling and finally going down with an appropriately powerful burn.

Setting his glass down, he shook his head and turned on his computer. As it loaded, he let his mind wander as the first hint of a buzz crept up on him.

For years, Lupine Freedom had been a shadow organization and true to its nature, it worked behind the scenes, quietly installing shifters into high positions among the police, governments and high society. Its funds came mostly from illicit drugs, at least, in the beginning; cocaine paid very well, as did gun running. Their goals at first had been to control society through subversion, to drum up the spirit of the downtrodden and turn them into weapons for power and control. Control, that when properly applied, would allow Rakinos to direct it towards his own ends which mainly consisted of the complete submission of anyone he felt was weaker and that, he thought sardonically, was a long list.

Rakinos, through proxies and using pawns (people who were angry with the world, angry at how it treated them because they weren't human enough), had selective news stories ran, articles and opinion pieces in the largest papers; first in the New York Times and later, as the internet took off, through online message boards. At last, the group had settled here in Dawson City and it was here, that Rakinos felt that Lupine Freedom had truly flourished. The late 1990s and early 2000s had been particularly fruitful for those ventures.

The city itself was fertile ground for suffering. The people in the lower east and west sides were poor and miserable. The rich puffed themselves up, like cocks of the walk, shitting down upon anyone below them and called it trickle-down economics. By the early 2000s, his reputation as a genetics expert in the field of lycanthropes was tarnished by several journalists that got a tad too close to the truth, ruining years of work. Of course, he wondered if any of the journalists' parts had ever been found. He doubted it. He checked from time to time and the last time he checked them, the cases had gone cold.

2002, he thought, had been one of their rougher years. That year, he had started to branch out into the more local opiate and black-market pill trade for funding as well as to make connections to the local shifter undergrounds, pushing the boundaries of his empire out into Carsonville, the wart on Dawson City's ass. He had found that like most medium size cities, Carsonville was built upon a foundation of conservative values. With that came plenty of Jesus, and with Jesus tended to come angry, hateful people who hated anyone who wasn't like them or who refused to conform. The shifter community in Carsonville was very subdued compared to Dawson City, with a few exceptions who didn't give a damn.

Rakinos had pulled the strings in that community, using the undercurrent of prejudice and fear, cutting here, connecting there. Before long he had built a decent sized trackway through Carsonville, using it as a shipping point for his drugs and guns to distribute. Downcast and angry, outcast shifters flocked to him and soon, the ranks of Lupine Freedom swelled, including the addition of John Carrey.

Rakinos took another deep drink and smiled, his red eyes simmering as he entered his password and let the biometric scanner read his iris.

With a beep and a whir, the computer began to work.

John Carrey had been angry, and Rakinos liked that. Angry was an understatement. John was young and angry and the fact that he was a walking tank was even better. Carrey had been a fighter for money and Rakinos had found him one night while scouting for recruits in the basement of an old, forgotten boxing dojo. The fights were organized by shifters who needed an outlet for their frustration, especially those less inclined to legal options. They were brutal and bloody with many shifters earning scars that took years to heal. The only rules in the fight club were no killing and no weapons.

Otherwise, anything was allowed and Rakinos had seen John, with his broad shoulders, blue-black fur and rage filled yellow eyes, win many matches. He was savage in the ring; he didn't dance around with his opponent, and that was a valuable trait in an enforcer. Fights were not dances; they weren't choreographed movie sequences. Fights were life or death and Carrey seemed to know that instinctively. Rakinos had watched him break limbs, knock teeth out, and bloody his opponent so fast that the other guy (or girl, he wasn't picky) was often down before they knew what had fallen upon them.

Carrey had been so full of rage that Rakinos barely had to persuade him. When Rakinos told him his plans for shifter superiority, Carrey had taken off his shirt and brushed back the fur on his left side, revealing a deep ugly brand of twisted scars.

He had been branded by a local religious group.

It had been easy to use that rage, to manipulate it in different ways, using various methods, to feed it and nurture it. Carrey had now been by his side ever since, for several years. Carrey had been the leader of the attack that Rakinos had staged on the Library of Congress, and ever since he had managed to get himself caught, Rakinos had been distant with him, despite staging a massive and quite bloody prison break as Carrey was being transferred. Failure could not be tolerated.

Failure, Rakinos thought calmly, studying his drink, often came in waves and that made him consider the past again, specifically a series of events that had stuck in his memory for a long time and only now, with Brian MacGregor's existence, did they really come to have significance.

A few years after John had joined them, something happened that, given recent events, Rakinos thought, was suspicious. There was a small group of shifters that had sought him out at the fight rings and had expressed an interest in joining. They said they had heard he was recruiting for an organization and that they had connections to local crack dealers who could help him facilitate his transport in and out of Carsonville. If what they said was true, it would have made for a windfall for Lupine Freedom in terms of cash.

One of them had been a male shifter with black fur and green eyes. He never shifted out of his wolf form and had said he was a full generation werewolf. The fellow seemed to be the leader of the little band and the new group, consisting of the black furred male, a brown furred male and a single tawny female shifter, all full generations, had served well for months. It was rare for so many full generations to assemble like that and Rakinos found it odd, given how rare the genetic defect was, but he took them at their word. They helped with several operations, including some enforcement missions before finally something happened that Rakinos found hard to ignore. John had been suspicious and one day had stormed into his office, his face livid.

John thrown down a newspaper onto the table that Rakinos had been working on, snarling in anger.

"We've got a problem."

Rakinos remembered looking up at Carrey in surprise for his boldness but when his right hand spoke, he usually listened; after all, he had molded the man well. He had pushed aside his work ups on trans-genetics and looked up.

"What?"

Carrey wasted no time, his ears flat against his skull as he snarled the words.

"Those guys we brought on a while back. At least one of them is a cop."

Rakinos had picked up the paper off the equations he had been working on and read the article. It was a community puff piece about the town's history. In it, the author had talked about the history of the chemical plant, its effect on the local economy and of course, its positive impact on the city, despite the fact that for the first ten years of its operation it essentially poisoned the river and thus people's drinking water. He had skimmed down, finally seeing what Carrey was talking about.

There it was. He read fast.

".....Carsonville may seem like a sleepy little city but has in fact an adrenaline filled past with the Carsonville Motor Rockets, a motocross racing stunt team that was started in 1951 by Robert Alderman. The team competed in several interstate competitions and its ris-

ing star was Jacob MacGregor, a young lycanthrope born and raised right here in town. Mac-Gregor was known for his daring stunts and break neck racing skills, bringing the team many trophies, including the regional championship in 1990.

For reasons only known to him, the next year, MacGregor, much to the chagrin of his teammates, retired from racing and has since become a local fixture in Carsonville City Police Department, moving through the ranks quickly and now serves as a dedicated and trusted detective..."

As Rakinos had read, he remembered John's deep voice growling low as he spoke. John didn't need to speak. The photo of the shifter in the article dressed in his black racing jacket with red and white stripes, waving his helmet proudly, his fur gleamed black with his unique green eyes was more than enough to confirm Carrey's own suspicions.

"I already did some digging. I tracked down the reporter. She told me that he's still a cop and I ran the names the other two gave me. Fakes. We've got pigs in the house, Rakinos. We need to fix this now."

Rakinos had looked up from the paper. *"The reporter?"*

"They'll find her body in a week or two I'd imagine if the river doesn't carry it too far. She tried to call the police."

Shaking his head, Rakinos had told Carrey to bring all three of them to him. Immediately.

2005 was an interesting year, Rakinos thought. Very interesting indeed. Carrey had been right of course and after he disposed of the cops, he exposed a larger sting operation underway and had promptly eliminated every single potential leak he could find. He found several leaks, and not just cops; there were also some eager young shifters trying to make new alliances with local gangs. In the end, he had them all killed with the help of John as his muscle.

Jake MacGregor had died last as Rakinos had finally reached a point of suspicion that not even John was above reproach and in a final test of loyalty, Rakinos had made sure that John proved his allegiance by executing the officer. MacGregor had stood defiant until the end, stoic and steady.

Rakinos had almost gone after the man's family, a human woman and human son, but John had persuaded him otherwise, reminding him that they needed to move, having already been compromised so badly. They had quickly packed up and shut down the operation in Carsonville, retreating to the safety of Dawson City, having learned a valuable lesson about carefully screening recruits, especially if they seemed to be angry or eager.

On his desk, the computer finally unlocked all the files for him that he had asked for and he already knew what he would find as he pulled up Brian Macgregor's file.

Not so human a child after all, Rakinos thought, amused by the strange connections life seemed to relish throwing at him.

As he stared at the information, he thought Brian was such an average person, that it was a miracle that MacGregor hadn't killed himself out of boredom. He was glad to finally put two and two together; who knew that a random cop he had killed years ago would have turned out to be the father of the very object of his scientific desire now? Had he gone through with eliminating the loose ends all those years ago before Brian had been turned....

Rakinos grunted under his breath as he read the files, thinking about the amazing power of coincidence... or was it fate?

Ever since he had been asked by Draco to help analyze Brian's situation, ever since he had heard the name *MacGregor*, Rakinos had felt a tickle of memory and it had taken days since Draco had first contacted him for it to finally surface. Now that it had, he felt that it was deliciously ironic that the cop that nearly exposed them had been also the same person to gift them with the greatest weapon Rakinos could ever have known.

The son himself, as Rakinos previously thought upon meeting him, was boring. He scrolled through the background checks.

MacGregor had become a security guard at a local hospital after not being able to cut college; He had tried to go after a degree in Criminal Justice but had dropped out a few years in. Reasons given were personal and Rakinos suspected that it was daddy issues, which made him roll his eyes. The boy was weak, then. Brian had established himself as something of a writer over the years, though nothing he had ever written had been published on a large scale, mostly the local paper and usually around Halloween. The boy had a taste for folklore and mystery.

He had some combat training in kendo and taekwondo, but he had dropped out of that too. He lived in a tiny one-bedroom apartment and had no connection to shifter politics or society until just these past few weeks when he had apparently made the mistake of doing his job. Pulling some strings at the local hospital, Rakinos had leaned on his contacts once he had left the manor with his stolen samples to find out more about Brian MacGregor and how he came to be.

In their drive to help MacGregor, they never realized just how much damage they were doing. Rakinos chuckled. Raven and Draco had foolishly told him all they knew up until that point. It served him well and now, Rakinos was able to put the puzzle together.

Two weeks ago, a man had come into the local hospital suffering from some kind of extreme overdose. Rakinos now knew that it had been one of the 86ers who had gotten into some of his stolen product, thanks to a certain young shifter who now served as the prototype for the Dog Soldiers. Brian and another guard had taken the human man down and had him arrested and as it turned out, Rakinos thought amused, the man himself had ironically been one of the original dealers that Alex had contacted. The 86ers were making a hefty profit from the leaked Bane and hadn't taken it too lightly when one of their top dealers was knocked out of the game by a glorified set of rent-a-cops.

The arresting officer had been on the take, of course, Rakinos mused, seeing the officer's name and connections. Ronson. Ronson had alerted his gang bosses looking for a reward. The gang had sent enforcers after both Brian and the other guard, Elijah Connors. Connors hadn't survived. Apparently he had put up fight and his body had been left broken, burned and branded. But Brian...

That's where Max Mullen came in it seemed like, Rakinos thought. From the information Draco and Raven had told him when he arrived to help her test the samples, Max had leveled the enforcers and had in an act of desperation to save Brian's life, bitten him. The enzymes in shifter saliva that normally should have shredded Brian's DNA on the spot (Rakinos thought back to Calvin with a satisfied grin, feeling his bourbon), had instead, activated a set of dormant shifter genetics.

In so doing, a truly interesting and powerful set of changes had been unleashed, the likes of which Rakinos had never seen anywhere before or since.

Brian's unique triple helix DNA and his unique projected ability to turn normal humans into shifters was a resource unlike any other, and Rakinos fully intended to convert Brian to his cause, by force if needed, or simply take what he wanted. Brian's DNA could be used to alter existing shifters and allow them to tolerate the destructive power of the Bane, making them into living super soldiers, the dream of the failed military years ago made manifest. If Rakinos could turn him, he could have a valuable weapon that could create more weapons and converts. If he couldn't, he would still have a resource as long as Brian lived and there were ways to keep someone in agony but alive at the same time for a long period. Rakinos had perfected those, especially for shifters with heightened immune systems. It took quite a bit to overwhelm them and Rakinos knew just far to take the line and dial it back before ramping it up again. Of course, if he outlived his usefulness...

As for Max Mullen....

Rakinos felt the red swirl of anger and the past swim up behind his eyes. He moved the mouse and pulled up all the information he had on Max Mullen.

The DNA tests did not lie and Rakinos now knew the truth, he simply had to draw the connections where they were.

He stared the screen, his red eyes sharp and for a while, they fell back to the past, his own this time as he connected the dots between them.

Rakinos himself had been born in 1970, and what a year it had been. Nixon had ordered an invasion of Cambodia, pushing the tensions even higher in Vietnam. Much the distress of fans around the world, the Beatles broke up. Mullen had been born in 1979, nine years later, almost a decade apart.

Rakinos had a near photographic memory and in his mind, he remembered his parents' names as if they were engraved in stone.

Eric and Diane Clairmont.

There were no Mullens. Not at first.

He sneered. Their last name, Clairmont, meant bright, shining, clear of sight and hearing and with a surge of hate and pride, he thought, it was ironic that they never saw what was coming for them before it was too late. Not that they were evil people, he admitted; they weren't. They were simply a young couple, not married, unprepared for the strain and commitment of having a child. Especially one that was born of a union that at the time was frowned on, between shifter and human, let alone a child with a rare mutation that locked them in their wolf form.

1970 had been a year indeed for the Clairmonts.

He knew his mother had received death threats from anonymous mailers, and once from a neighbor, Rakinos himself had been the target. He had been three and a half when the neighbor called him a mutt. Rakinos, already talking early, had asked what a mutt was and his mother had told him to pay that angry man no mind.

He also knew his father tried as best as he could to shield them all from the vitriol being slung their way. By the time Rakinos was four, already big for his age and highly intelligent, he had gained a reputation for being what some would call a prob-lem child, albeit a quiet one. His parents desperately tried to contain his... *hobbies*.

His parents consistently found dead animals in their yard, sometimes buried, sometimes not. The animals were ravaged, while others were found with surgical cuts. Rakinos remembered his father having to put one of the poor squirrels out of its misery.

Neither his mother or his father blamed him outright; perhaps they were afraid as well. Both of them kept a wary eye on him and soon he had to keep his side hobbies more discrete, learning early the art of deception. It wasn't easy. His mother was very perceptive for a human and his father, with his werewolf hearing, sight and smell was even harder to get past.

By the time he was school age, Rakinos was already in several fights a day.

When he was seven, the neighbor that had called him a mutt soon found his favorite pet cat (one of at least ten) hung from his clothesline, its guts strung out and laid in piles below it, spelling "mutt."

Of course, that neighbor had accused Rakinos, citing him as *"the only demented little shit cruel enough to do it and he would press charges, just you wait!"*

The charges never came.

A week later, the neighbor had a very unfortunate accident while working on his lawnmower. Somehow, the thing had suddenly revved to life and the blades, well, *perhaps he should have taken them off before crawling up under the damn thing*, Rakinos thought darkly. He had watched as the police had come up a few hours later after the mailman found the chopped remains. The entire side of the white house and fence had been painted a very pretty shade of cherry red, even with the little grey lumps in it.

The police never questioned him, thinking instead that it was a simple electrical malfunction and a careless owner.

Rakinos had watched them cart off what remained of the neighbor in a bucket covered in black plastic.

It was then that he found he enjoyed the scent of blood, enjoyed how it flowed. It was such a beautiful fluid in how it coated whatever it touched.

Not long after that, his mother had begun to watch him even more carefully, so carefully in fact that he had to leave his animals alone and that made him angry. The urges and rage inside of him were forced to be contained, to be measured. It bottled up inside him like a pressure cooker. He was a big kid for his age and he knew he was stronger than anyone else was...stronger than his parents were. He could take care of them if he wanted but he held back; something about his mother and his father held him in check and he hated them for it. He couldn't explain it and then one day he realized it was.

He was afraid of taking that final step.

That realization had enraged him to the point that he hadn't even slept that night it occurred to him, the thoughts chasing him round and round in the darkness, hounding him. The next morning, he had not spoken to either one of his parents and had gone to school. For most of the day, things had been fine.

Then there was that kid.

What was his name? Rakinos, thought and then it came to him, floating out of the crimson mist of his mind as he took another hit from the strong drink.

Donny Tellerson.

Donny was a fat kid, a bullied victim as much as he was the bully himself. He took out his rage on anyone and anything he could get his hands on. Rakinos and everyone else knew his father was a lazy drunk and there were stories that his mom worked the sidewalk café, where any john could place an order if he could pay. An ugly kid with a round face and mousy ratty brown hair and beady wet eyes, Donny had consistently picked on Rakinos since day one and that day was no different, at least for Donny.

For Rakinos, it was a very different day indeed because it was that day that he killed fear and unleashed the rage he had pent up at being supervised like a hawk. All that pent-up anger and frustration and the dark impulses he had been forced to keep in check finally exploded.

Donny had pushed him in the back, sending him sprawling to the ground hard. Rakinos remembered his muzzle striking the white tile and the sharp pain as his nose shot blood all over the floor. There were no teachers around. Donny was careful when he chose his moments. The other kids had all stood back, all of them watching to see what would happen, shifters and human children alike.

Rakinos at first had been stunned and then as he opened his eyes and looked down and he saw his own red blood on the floor, the safety valve that he had crudely fashioned on his inner hellish self at last fully gave way as he wiped his red furred hand across his face and got to his knees, standing up and turning around to face a leering Donny who was slinging insults at him like bullets.

Rakinos remembered feeling none of them. All he saw was Donny's round fat face with the one pimple that was growing in under his left eye. He remembered feeling something inside of him give way, like a dam bursting and it felt wonderful. He felt his fear die and in its place something new rose like a bat winged, shadowy monster and he welcomed it.

He punched Donny in the face with all his might, instantly breaking Donny's nose with a wet crunch.

With a spray of blood and snot, Donny had stumbled backward, letting out a high-pitched scream of pain and shock.

Rakinos simply moved in and shoved him backward squarely in the chest. Donny had stumbled harder, nearly losing his footing. Rakinos fixed that situation for him quickly. He lashed out with a powerful kick, sending Donny sprawling into a crying heap onto the floor with a wet smack of a fleshy body hitting cold unforgiving tile.

"Whut fa fubk bude...." Donny had cried, his voice slurred, his face and hands a crimson mess.

Rakinos said nothing but stood over him, his scarlet eyes looking over Donny's ankle.

A lesson needed to be taught here. Respect would not be earned but it would be taken.

Rakinos slammed his foot down on Donny's ankle, snapping it like a wet toothpick.

The bone exploded through the skin in a compound fracture and a second later, the fat kid's ankle stuck out at an extremely unnatural angle. The scream that he let out was beyond inhuman; it was agony, and to Rakinos, it sounded like music. He wanted to hear more of it, needed more of it. Donny hadn't learned yet. But he would; oh yes, he would.

Kicking Donny's ruined ankle aside, Rakinos fell upon him, beating him in the face, the ribs, the neck, the ears, anywhere he could reach, his powerful fists fell, red fur soon turning dark with wet warm blood. He heard bones crunch, heard the sickening sound of his fist striking thick fatty flesh over and over. He relished it. To him it was a dance with death, and one he had longed for after weeks of being cooped up. This was more than a lesson, Rakinos had thought. This was fun.

Donny's screams ripped up and down the halls and he fought back or tried to. Rakinos broke his wrist for his efforts and two ribs for the trouble. Rakinos could see the teachers coming down the hall, running, their features fully shadowed by the afternoon light.

Blow after blow fell and soon, he thought that Donny's face, cracked and bleeding, with bone sticking out of his shattered eye socket, looked much better this way and eventually Donny stopped fighting back and instead fell still, his cries of pain slowing to nothing as the teachers finally yanked Rakinos off of him.

Rakinos distinctly remembered seeing the results of his rage, the broken bloody boy on the floor who's face and body may have had better luck with a speeding truck. He remembered feeling the rush of excitement. The thrill of it. It made his heart pound, his blood rush in his ears, his red eyes had dilated as a type of euphoria came over him.

The rest of that afternoon went by in a haze as the police were called, ambulances had come and taken Donny away.

His mother had pulled him from school that day and did not allow him back. Rakinos heard Diane (he no longer thought of her as his mother) talking to someone on the phone as she wept to Eric who tried to comfort her. Straining, Rakinos had been able to pick up the phone conversation, his red ears swiveling.

Donny Tellerson was comatose and paralyzed from the waist down. If he ever woke up, he wouldn't walk again for the rest of his life.

Rakinos smiled. Good. That's what happened to people who treated him like that. He would never put up with it again. Sometime later, he recalled hearing that Donny had died in his sleep.

For the next few days, his parents had left him alone and then one afternoon a week after the incident in school, they had asked him to come downstairs, that they needed to talk to him.

Rakinos remembered walking down those stairs and seeing two men in white shirts and white pants and a woman with iron gray hair tied up into a bun. She looked severe in her dark suit and knee length skirt and her eyes tracked him as he moved. All three of them were human, at least as far as he could tell.

Diane and Eric together told him that he needed help and the best way they knew to do that is to let these people take him for a while, to see if they could help him back on his feet and to find his way. That they felt they couldn't help him at home and that it was best for them all.

The two men in white had stepped forward towards Rakinos and he had warily stepped back. He didn't care about his parents but he wasn't going with those people. They would not take his freedom.

He had tried to turn and run, thinking of ten thousand ways to escape but they were bigger than he was, stronger too, if that was possible. They had him in moments, pinning his arms in such a way as that he could get no leverage at all. They stayed clear of his teeth as well. He felt something sharp prick his neck and he suddenly found that his strength had failed him but his rage did not fail.

He watched Diane cry as they took him out the front door; he watched Eric hold her close and close his eyes, turning away from his ranting son, his son that was screaming at them that he would not forget this and that one day he would come back for them, just like Donny because they were just like Donny.

Rakinos had spent the next years of his life in The Center, which was its name as well as function. It was a psychiatric hospital that specialized in treating violent patients, patients with histories gory enough and tragic enough that Rakinos just fit right in. Where it was located, he couldn't tell. They never let him see the roads going to it, that way in case of escapes, the escapee wouldn't know which way to go and given the histories of many of their patients, it was best that they didn't.

At first, they had tried counseling, one on one with a therapist. His therapist was a young human woman with gentle brown eyes and a calm voice. She seemed eager to genuinely help him and get to the root of his "problem" as they called it. She was never rude to him, never mean, never demeaning. For months she had tried to get him to open up and even in failure, she was polite to him. She was one of the few who was kind.

It enraged him. To be shackled down and subjected to that useless prattle. There was nothing wrong with him. It was the way he was, simple as that. He knew he was different, but he didn't consider it a fault. Instead, since being taken from his parents, given up by their weakness, he had found a curious strength in his solitude. There were also monsters within the facility and as he endured them, he embraced the darkness within and found that he was never lonely again. He remembered thinking that, the older he got, the darker red his fur became, like blood and it had become a source of pride for him.

One day, during a therapy session, after months at the hands of the orderlies, something his therapist had said set off a spark and he managed to get one of his hands lose and waited.

When the therapy session was over, the therapist in all her gentility, lay quite dead, her eyes gouged out and her tongue pinned to the roof of her mouth with a screw that he had managed to rip loose from the metal table. Her prattle was silenced and he never again accepted or tolerated pity. Her death was an abject lesson that it too was weakness.

It was after that that the drugs started; the injections. The serums and of course, their favorite, electroshock therapy; oh boy they loved that last one. They said it would cause short term memory loss and maybe that was what the doctors were hoping for, to erase some of him so he couldn't hurt anyone again but they failed.

He remembered it all and it was the early days of shifter medicine so they had no sedatives to give him, no pain killers that would work.

Rakinos remembered the buzzing whine of the ECT machine as it ramped up and remembered the cold touch of the metal paddles against his temples, the blazing hot fire that exploded in his body's nerve endings. They had no idea at the time that shifters had an intricate nervous system that responded to electrical stimulation far differently from a baseline humans. It was agony beyond description.

He remembered the one orderly who could carry his limp body back to his room to be locked up, Jason Ruger. Ruger was a big brawny human man with mean eyes. He was not known to be kind to the patients and had dark appetites that he satisfied on the more comatose ones, the ones who could never tell, the ones who couldn't form words and instead drooled themselves senseless every day.

Ruger had turned his appetites on young Rakinos early on, the shame keeping the young werewolf quiet. After Rakinos killed his therapist, things got even worse, because Rakinos had been truly powerless to fight back and that was when Ruger really doubled down, taking a liking to the young shifter. Rakinos remembered Rugers' big meaty human hands moving down his red furred chest, sliding down and under the waistband of his hospital issue paper pants. Rakinos remembered the shame, the hate and the anger as he was left alone, unable to move, his pants wet and his belly fur sticky. He had cried then, but they were tears of rage as his body refused to comply with his commands, still reeling from the ECT. His parents had abandoned him because they were weak and sentenced him to hell. He made up his mind after being left lying like that one night that if this was hell, he would rule it.

Ruger himself had an accident one year later and ended up a patient in his own ward as he seemed to have been overdosed on something that fried his brain. He spent the rest of his days eating pureed peas, crying because he didn't like the apricots on Friday. The accident was never explained though of course, none of the patients complained.

Rakinos himself eventually learned that if he pretended to go along with whatever they wanted of him, he got freedoms and so, over a period of years, he continued to do just that until finally, in 1996, he managed to get himself released with a brand-new lease on life, declared sane and allowed to walk again in the sun for the first time in what felt like a lifetime. To the doctors, he put on a mask he had crafted over the years, a mask of sanity and peace, of rational discourse and well thought out conversations.

The first thing he did was go to his parents' house.

They were gone, having moved a long time ago.

For a time, he searched and had nearly given up, turning his attention to his growing interest into the study of genetics and lycanthropic biology. He intended to earn his degree, his hateful urges contained for a while, and then one day, he overheard a conversation at a local restaurant where he had come to get a bite while studying. Two redneck idiots were sitting side by side, drinking bad coffee. They had been talking about local people, local history and Rakinos, up until now, had tried to ignore them until they said something that truly caught his attention.

"Say you heard about that crazy kid?"

"No, what crazy kid?"

"Back in the seventies. They say he was a mutant, a werewolf or something. Beat a local boy to death when he was seven. Word is he may have murdered a fellow. Parents sent him up to The Center or some shit."

"No shit...whatever happened to them?"

"Not a goddamned clue. I heard stories that they changed their names and moved away. I sure as hell would if I gave birth to some little freak like that..."

That single lead had sparked his quest to find them anew and this time he checked local records before threatening the life of a local clerk and he learned quickly that applied fear could be very useful. She gave him the records he needed and he killed her quickly for it, striking out for Alaska that winter, his violent urges finally released and he channeled them into his quest for revenge.

Eric and Diane Clairmont had married and changed their names to Mullen.

There was no mention of him, he noticed. He did find out that his parents had legally surrendered him to the state not long after The Center had come to pick him up, apparently at the suggestion of the state. They were weak then and were hiding now. He had scared them badly and they knew that he was capable of getting his revenge, just like he promised that day in their living room, which is why they had run. Of course, they could have felt shame from their decision but no, Rakinos thought. It had been fear. Fear of him. It could be nothing else.

Mullen.

Rakinos flicked his eyes to the screen, looking at a snapshot of Max Mullen's gray furred face and his blue eyes from security footage from a street camera.

Diane's eyes.

In the winter of 1996, Rakinos had spent weeks locating them and finally found them in Alaska. He had watched them for days, and then as the heaviest snowfall of the year began, he had made his move.

Eric had fallen first, ridiculously easy. Rakinos still remembered the words he whispered to his father as he died.

*"I always keep my promises, **dad**. Just like you taught me. Proud?"*

Of course, their new son had been there, all of seventeen and in a rage, had tried to stop him, and Rakinos had simply knocked him back across the yard. Rakinos never knew the kid's name. Thinking he had hit the teen hard enough to kill him, Rakinos relished remembering as in his mind, he broke down the front door, walked into the kitchen and turned on the gas stove, letting the blue-orange jets reach high, and in moments, the curtains were in flame and that flame spread quickly.

As he had walked through his parent's house and he had taken stock of what their life had become after changing their name from Clairmont to Mullen.

Happy family memories of ski trips. Science fair projects. Shining pictures of Diane and Eric with their new son as he celebrated a birthday, his first lost tooth. In one of them, the young gray furred child was with Eric, both werewolves happily working on an engine while Diane obviously took the photo. The young werewolf, covered in grease, held up a wrench much to Eric's proud pleasure.

It was sickeningly sweet and it also bothered him for some reason that he couldn't pinpoint at first and then when he did, it made him even angrier. It was jealousy.

They had replaced him, like he was nothing, proving that he was right all those years ago, that his parents were really no different that Donny Tellerson. They never cared. He knew it. They would learn the same lesson he taught Donny.

By the time Rakinos had cornered his mother, she was begging him, pleading, not because of her own need to live but for son. *Give him the chance you couldn't take, the one you never had because we failed you! We tried to help you! Don't punish him for our mistakes!* she had screamed at him and Rakinos had slit her throat without a second thought and stabbed her with the knife he had with him.

He hated mewling.

At that moment, that grey furred teenager had come up the stairs, blooded but alive, and Rakinos could hear the safety valves on the propane tanks beginning to fail and so, knowing what was to become of them all very soon, left his mother to bleed out and the brother he never wanted to die.

He remembered leaping out of the window, crashing into the snow and watching from afar as the house went up in a fireball, consuming everything around it before it collapsed into a burning hulk.

By 2018, Rakinos had pushed all thoughts of Eric and Diane Clairmont, later Mullen, from his mind; they no longer mattered. Their unknown son also no longer mattered. He was a nameless son, a corpse that had been incinerated in the conflagration with the rest of his bastard family. When a certain gray werewolf carrying a mutation much like his own that blocked him from being able to shift began beating up thugs, some of his own men included in that number, Rakinos didn't make the connection. Now, things had changed. Drastically.

As it turns out, he thought, that nameless son did in fact, have a name.

Max.

He had even met Max, face to face so to speak, in 2013 at one of Draco's final rallies, the one that was broken up by a human caused riot, the same one that ended up claiming Barbara Riley's life. What Rakinos had told Ash, had in fact, not been entirely true. Rakinos had started the riot and engaged with the anti-werewolf protestors to prove a point, to show Draco how wrong he was, that humans could not be trusted. That peace was a lie and that act had cost the Riley's their sister. Rakinos had pulled the trigger himself and blamed a rogue human, letting the man take the fall. Of course, the man had witnessed Rakinos take the shot and so Rakinos had to clean up loose ends. It had all been designed to break Draco and drive him out of the public eye, at least at rallies, to weaken his resolve. Draco was spreading hope and Lupine Freedom could not flourish if there was hope. Of course, to the public and to the police, it was just a situation that had gotten out of hand and Draco and Ash and their family, not even Max, really knew the truth though Max held him responsible.

The man was no fool but without evidence...

Rakinos' face darkened.

But now, as his past finally came full circle, Rakinos looked at the image of Max Mullen on screen and saw his father's ghost and his mother's eyes in the brother he thought long dead. Now that that brother was no longer a nameless charred corpse but rather a very much alive and well reminder of the one thing Rakinos hated more than any other: *failure.*

Even though he now knew that Max was his brother, Rakinos wondered if Max knew it. Probably not. Eric and Diane evidently never told him. Perhaps, it was time to change that, Rakinos thought as he sat back in his chair, finishing off the last of his bourbon.

In fact, he could kill two birds with one stone. He could simultaneously take Brian MacGregor and utterly break Max Mullen and finish what he started years ago.

He picked up the phone on his desk and dialed a number. After a moment, John Carrey's deep voice came over the end.

Rakinos smiled, almost purring.

"John, I have a job for you. I need you to find out where Max Mullen and Brian MacGregor are at this moment and then tell me. Do not engage them and do not let them see you. Simple recon."

"Will do."

Rakinos killed the line and sat back to think long and hard in the quiet darkness in which his red eyes glowed like hellish coals.

CHAPTER 2

It was just before eleven thirty in the morning at Chris MacGregor's house.

The daylight had brought with it a warmth that Chris hadn't seen or a felt in her house in a very long time. She had awoken well before Brian or Max, and she wondered if they had slept well after they finally went back to bed. She had showered, cleaned herself up and even had her cup of coffee before she even thought to go and check on the two of them. She went upstairs and gave the door a quick knock.

She heard shuffling and a moment later, Brian's sleep choked voice called out and she smiled. It was just like having him back at home again, taking her back years to his teenage days.

".... We're alive...I think..." she heard him grunt through the door.

Chris smiled. "Good. Come downstairs when you guys are ready. I made breakfast for lunch."

"Roger that..." Brian said back through a cavernous yawn.

In the bedroom, Brian was on his back, his eyes crusty with sleep as he blinked it away to see the white ceiling, feeling the sun's warmth pushing through the closed blinds on the window. He stretched his toes out under the blanket and felt that his tail had gone numb. Frowning, he didn't know that could happen and raised his butt up a bit off the bed and tried to move his tail to get blood flow back into it; with a rush of pins and needles, it did.

"Man, that feels weird..." he said to himself more than anything else. He glanced over at Max and saw that Max was still sleeping.

Brian let himself glance over Max's sleeping form, and just let everything else go. Max's eyes were closed and he wasn't curled over into a fetal position. He was breathing slow and steady. His eyes barely moved behind his eyelids.

Whatever he's seeing, I hope it's not a nightmare again, Brian thought. He seemed very peaceful, tranquil even. Brian reached over and laid a gentle hand on Max's right shoulder and gave it a small shake.

A moment later, Max grunted and opened his blue eyes, blinking owlishly at Brian.

"Hey...what's up..." he said his voice husky from sleep.

Brian smiled. "Not much but take a whiff of the air."

Frowning, Max did. "All I smell is us."

Brian saw a tiny sleepy grin form on his muzzle. He gave him a playful shove.

"Smell again."

Max did, inhaling deeply. Instantly his eyes widened and he woke up completely.

"Is that.... sausage and eggs? Bacon and toast?"

Brian nodded. "It is. Mom came up and said she made breakfast for lunch. She's not done that in a while." He drug himself up into a sitting position and kicked the blankets off himself.

He yelped in pleasant surprise a moment later as he felt Max's brawny arms come around him and pull him back in the bed playfully.

Landing on Max's chest, Brian looked up into Max's eyes and smiled at Max's devilish grin.

"Where do you think you're going?" Max asked mischievously. Brian grunted and laughed a bit as he tried to get up but Max was stronger, at least right now; because honestly, Brian didn't want to get up just yet even though he had to.

"Going to go stuff my face with that food downstairs."

Max leaned down into Brian's ear and growled softly. "I know something else we could stuff our faces with."

Brian lost it, laughing heartily. "Get out of this bed with me and let's go downstairs before you talk me into something that's going to get us both in trouble."

Max was smiling warmly at him, their noses almost touching.

"I guess that sounds like a good idea. You gonna tell your mom about finally being able to shift?"

"Not yet. I want to keep that to myself for a while."

Brian reached up and touched noses with Max gently, unsure of why he did it but it felt right, better and more impish than a kiss. As he did, he actually licked Max nose full on with his tongue, like a dog, and didn't know why he did that either. It just felt right.

That surprised Max enough to get the bigger shifter to let him go and sent Max into a small fit of what was for him, the closest thing he could get to laughter.

"And I have no idea why I just did that but okay then." Brian said with a giggle snort, standing up off the bed, glad to be moving. His back was a bit stiff.

Max looked him as he stood there drinking in Brian's muscled body, his black fur just drinking in the sunlight like a black hole. He found his eyes tracing down following his tail line, past the round firmness of Brian's butt and Max found himself grinning like a kid.

Brian felt the stare.

He turned and raised an eyebrow. "So that's why I felt like a piece of beef jerky."

Max snorted. "Please..."

Brian grinned. "It is nice though. Being appreciated. It's been a while. Well, ever is a better estimate."

Max nodded, taking his time with his eyes. "It's...very... nice." With that, Max turned over on his back and Brian laughed as he saw the blankets were tented up in cone just below Max's waist.

"I think I'm a bad influence on you," Brian joked as he grabbed his clothes off the floor. "While that goes down for you, I'm going to head to the bathroom and wash up my face and teeth. My mouth feels like scum, plus I've got the strong suspicion I've got a cow lick. Feel free to use anything in the bathroom. Towels are in the closet just outside the hall if you want to wash your face."

Brian turned to go out into the hallway standing in the open door. He felt Max staring at him from behind and he turned his head side to side, looking for his mom and when he was sure she wasn't there, he slid a finger into the cotton waistband of his trunks and slid them down, just enough expose his furry right butt cheek. He heard Max grunt behind him and a moment later a balled-up sock hit him in the back of the head.

Laughing to himself, he made for the bathroom to get woke up and try to get going for the day.

Fifteen minutes later, both Max and Brian had come downstairs, fully dressed. Instead of wearing the brown over shirt, Brian had tied its long sleeves around his waist. The cowlick had refused to go entirely away, he thought with a bit of embarrassment but he didn't really care when it came down to it. Max of course had managed to get the fur on his head to lay down and everything else that was messed up was covered by his shirt and pants. They had cleaned up the bedroom and made the bed before coming down and as they came around the corner into the kitchen, Chris looked up from her coffee in the living room.

"Hey boys, morning. Hope you got some rest. Food is on the counters. You know where the plates are, Brian. Help yourselves. I made plenty. I know how you big fellas eat." She said happily, going back to her coffee and the television which was currently turned to the news.

Looking at Max, Brian nodded towards the kitchen. "Let's dig in before I start eating it right out of the bowl."

Max agreed and when Brian started lifting the covers off the dishes, he felt his stomach leap in anticipation. His blue eyes widened.

"Wow, Chris....you went all out...thanks." Max said, his voice still a bit husky from sleep. Chris waved him off gently from the living room.

"Honey if you are going to be a part of this family you are going to learn that I love to cook. Thank god we've always had decent metabolisms otherwise we'd be fatter than a bunch of bears in winter. You're welcome, by the way."

Max smiled. He liked her. A lot.

Brian handed him a plate and together they both loaded up on scrambled eggs, toast, bacon strips and sausage patties. There were even a few of those little golden biscuits and some homemade country gravy. It sat in a bowl, grey with black pepper flecks and it made both of them growl with anticipation.

"Was that your stomachs?" Chris asked, bemused.

"No, just everything smells fantastic, mom. Thanks...we mean it. Damn." Brian replied, setting out glasses for himself and Max. He took orange juice while Max snagged a glass of milk. The two of them came over into the living room and sat down, their plates on their knees, forks in hand.

"Good! You got a real amount. So, how'd you sleep?"

As Brian dug in, Max swallowed a bit and told her. "Pretty good I guess. I usually have trouble sleeping anyway but honestly, it was a better sleep than I've had in long time."

Chris nodded approvingly. "Awesome. What do you guys have planned today?"

Now it was reversed with Max with a mouthful and Brian free.

"Not sure. We need to head back to the city. My paid leave is about up and need to take care of some things at the apartment."

Frowning, Chris asked, "How long have you been off work?"

Brian sheepishly told her.

"Two weeks? Good god, how did you convince them of that?"

Max chimed in with a knowing grin. "Apparently you are laid up with a nasty case of the flu and desperately needed home care."

Chris looked from Max to Brian and Brian nodded.

A moment later she burst out laughing. "Oh my god, you are awful. Well, it's a good thing I know so I can keep your story straight. Do you miss work?"

Brian had cleaned half his plate by this point and swallowed his drink carefully, thoughtfully.

"In a way, but in a way I don't. I'm not sure I'll be going back to the hospital."

Chris shook her head. "That's understandable, considering what you went through. Any ideas about where you'd like to end up?"

Brian shrugged. "I've been thinking. There's this club, The Wolves Den. Do you know it?"

Shaking her head, Chris told him no.

"Well, it's a really nice club and that's where I was taken to recover since I didn't want to go to the hospital. It's got a lower level that helps shifters and people like me get back on their feet, sort of like a high-tech halfway house. Draco's brother owns it. Might see if I can talk to him and see if he needs any help."

Chris smiled and leaned back into her chair. "You know...you are just like your dad. You both enjoyed helping people and protecting them."

Hearing that made Brian's face go warm and honestly, made him feel the tiniest surge of pride.

"Never thought about it like that. It is kind of odd that we both ended up doing similar work."

"Speaking of," Chris said, setting her coffee cup down on the table. "There's one more thing I want you to have of your dad's and I thought it for a while before I thought it was the right thing. I'll go get it."

Frowning, Brian watched her head out of the living room and down the hall, vanishing into her bedroom.

When they were alone, Max looked over at Brian. "You really thinking of asking Ash if he needs help?"

Brian nodded. "Yeah. I don't think I could go back to the hospital after all this. You guys did so much to help me even when I was stupid and I just can't explain it really. This whole life, you know...the shifter bit...was part of my dad's life and he gave it up for me. I think I want to explore it more. I think he'd want me to."

"Makes sense. Draco and Ash don't really speak much anymore but I can talk to Ash and see what he says. It would be good to have you closer, if I'm honest. Can't say I'd object." Max replied, his ears lowering a bit as he felt his face flush. Brian saw it and grinned. He agreed.

"It would be nice. Wish my apartment wasn't so far away."

Chris still hadn't come back yet and Max sat thoughtfully for a moment, quiet as he turned something over in his mind.

"Well, you know you can come over and stay anytime you want...I don't mind."

His words made Brian's ears perk up and he turned to look at Max who was wearing the sincerest expression Brian had ever saw him wear. Brian's mouth turned up in a smile.

"I'd like that."

"Good." Max said quietly and smiled himself, tucking away the last of his breakfast, and put his plate on top of Brian's, both of them feeling thoroughly stuffed. Something else seemed to occur to him and he looked up at Brian.

"Maybe if this works out...you could do more than just visit..." Max said quietly, almost sheepishly.

Brian thought about that. He liked that idea but didn't want to push things too far just yet. So far, it had been much smoother than he had anticipated and he didn't' want to jinx anything.

"Could be. We'll see but I like that idea. I really do." He said and laid a hand on Max's arm giving it a solid squeeze. Max seemed to perk up after that and Chris chose that moment to come back.

They both looked up as she came over to them and stood before Brian.

She was holding something in her hands, something on a fine silver chain.

"Brian this is very important to me and it was to your dad as well. It's got a lot of sentimental value behind it and I think he would have wanted you to have it. I do and I think it needs to be with you. It wasn't in the box because I like to keep it close."

She extended her hand and Brian held up his, the tips of his fur turning silvery as the sunlight passed through them. As she opened her hand, the silver chain fell and draped itself around his hand. There, on the chain, was a single silver ring. The ring itself was deeply engraved with Celtic ribbons and ancient designs. Inside of the band, Brian could make out curved writing.

To Jake, my love, always.

The ring itself looked like it would have fit his ring finger so it definitely wasn't for a human sized finger, at least, not a normal human sized finger. He realized it was a wedding ring.

"Mom..." Was all he could say as he stared at her in shock. He found that his voice was surprisingly small in that moment.

Chris closed her hand over his and clasped them together, the silver ring vanishing from sight as Brian's hand closed over it.

"This is your dad's real wedding ring, the one I got him when we first got married. He wore it in those pictures you saw but when we had you and he decided to stay in human form, we got him a different one that fit in his human form. This one always meant the most to him and to me. Take it and keep it with you, so that you always have a piece of him. Take that jacket too and the box." she said, nodding to a chair beside the front door. Brian glanced at it and saw his father's old motocross racing jacket had been cleaned and lay draped over the chair looking brand new. On the floor next to it was the box, taped back shut.

"Mom...wow....I don't know what to say."

Chris reached out and pulled his furry head to her and kissed him on the forehead.

"You don't have to say anything, my dear. I just know I'm proud to see you following in his footsteps, no matter what brought you here. You're strong, just like him and maybe a little like me. You and Max seem happy and that's all that matters to me. I want you to know your father like I did. Really know him."

With a contented and somewhat sad sigh, Chris made her way back to her chair as Brian opened his hand and looked down at the ring on the chain. He met Max's eyes for a moment and then placed the chain around his neck. Surprisingly, it was perfectly sized for him. It must have been one of his dad's old chains.

On the television, the President was on screen as a clip played from what the news ticker said was a press conference earlier that morning.

Brian listened to the words and felt something inside him stir.

The President stood behind a podium, in a dark suit with a red tie that was far too long, his skin glistening from sweat and a fake orange tan.

"We must protect ourselves and protect our families. I know that better than anyone, no one really knows protection like I do. If the vote passes on the registration act, I will make sure, this I promise you, that I will sign it into law as soon as it is on my desk and believe me, our country will be safer than it ever has before."

Brian felt his brows furrow and he gritted his teeth. A low growl formed in the back of his throat. He didn't like politics before, and he had always tried to steer clear of them, only offering an opinion if he was directly asked but now...

Now things were different. Now he had a stake in a fight he didn't have before and it was jarring to put it mildly. Suddenly, he knew what it was to feel the effect of something that would have flown over his head as he changed channels in his apartment or tuned that orange oaf out. Maybe, Brian thought, he should have been more involved to begin with, not just once it affected him.

"Why are people like him always the ones that get the most voice?" he asked rhetorically, disgusted.

"Because people are afraid and when they are afraid they do stupid things. People are angry and when they are angry, they do terrible things. Deep down, they're all afraid that they are losing their identity." Max said, a hint of sadness in his voice as he flicked his eyes from the TV to Brian. Brian looked over at him, genuinely surprised at such an insight.

"Yeah..."

"Surely it won't pass," Chris said. "There's no way they could enforce that nonsense. They'd have to set up blood testing centers around the country, hell, it would be a chaotic mess."

Brian nodded. "Maybe. Anyway, Max, think we should be hitting the road? It's going on fifteen to one. What time do you go to work, mom?"

Chris looked suddenly surprised. "Shit. I forgot that I did today. I go in at one. I'd better go and get the computer booted up. Boys don't worry about the mess. I'll clean it."

With that they all stood; Chris stepped up to Brian.

"I love you, honey. Come by more often. We have a lot to catch up on. I have so many stories to share with you."

Brian reached out and pulled her into a hug, burying his muzzle into her hair.

She smelled like strawberries and cream.

"I will. I promise. Love you, mom."

Chris moved over to Max and looked up at him.

"Thanks for everything, Chris. I don't get to do this kind of stuff often. Maybe I should. I don't exactly have a lot of family but--" He began and to his surprise, she hugged him too. Brian watched as Max stiffened and then relaxed into it, and for a moment, saw something flicker in Max's eyes and this time, Brian understood as a part of him hurt for Max, but warmed with the thought that maybe now he had something that had been lost to him for a while.

Max smiled though when the hug was done, even though his eyes were a tad moist. Thankfully, Chris didn't seem to notice.

"You're a good man, Max. I can tell you are hard on yourself, harder than you need to be. I don't know the full story but one day when you feel ready, you can tell me and I'll be here to listen. In the meantime, this is your home too. You're family. Take care of each other. Lean on each other. That's how'll you'll make in life." She said quietly.

Max nodded. "I will. I promise."

"Good! Now scoot I've got to get logged in before I'm late. Drive safe and I love you boys! Brian don't forget that jacket and the box!" she said and hurried over to her computer station and booted it up.

"You ready?" Max asked, reaching into his pocket for his keys. Brian nodded and reached into his own and handed Max back his socket.

Max shook his head. "Nah. Hold onto that. Keep it for a while."

Brian shrugged, touched by the gesture and not sure what to say.

"If you say so." He grinned.

On the way out, Brian scooped up the jacket and box. As they stepped out of the house, Brian looked back at his mom as she plugged in her headset and her fingers began to fly over the keyboard. He saw her as she truly was, he thought. He saw the lines under her eyes, the time that was slowly turning her hair lighter every year and saw how her joints hurt her more often.

The most horrifying thought ran through him and that thought was that if Draco was right, Brian himself would far outlive his mother. He would see her grow old as he remained just as he was now, frozen in time more or less; that thought sent a pang of fear through him and a cold glaze of sorrow.

For some reason, Brian got the horrible impression that this might be the last time he saw her and he had a hard time shaking it for a moment. He made a note to actively spend more time with her.

He felt Max tap his elbow and the touch snapped him out of his moment and for that, he was grateful. Closing the house door behind him, Brian and Max made for the truck and in a few minutes, they were back on the road, heading home to Dawson City, the jacket and box of memories in the back seat.

As they drove, Max's phone rang and looking at the road, he asked Brian to check who it was.

Brian picked up the phone from the dash console pocket and looked.

"Unknown caller."

Max shrugged. "Block it."

Brian slid his finger across the screen towards the red REJECT button and the phone stopped ringing.

"How about some music on the way home?" Max asked as he reached towards the radio.

"That would be awesome." Brian replied, putting the phone back into the console slot.

With a flick of the dial, Max's playlist started and the song made Brian laugh out loud.

"This is not what I expected at all!" he giggle snorted.

Max shot him a look with bemusement. "What, I have good taste in music."

Brian nodded. "Yeah, you do. It's just unexpected but not bad. Not bad at all."

The sounds of Electric Light Orchestra blasted out, shaking the windows and Brian bobbed his head to the music, his ears flopping just a bit at the tips and a moment later, Max although resisting at first, gave in and shook his head with him as they both badly sang a moment later.

Sun is shinin' in the sky

There ain't a cloud in sight

It's stopped rainin' everybody's in a play

And don't you know

It's a beautiful new day, hey hey

Runnin' down the avenue

See how the sun shines brightly in the city

On the streets where once was pity

Mister blue sky is living here today, hey hey

Brian's earlier fears melted away slowly and he realized that this was a pretty good day after all.

######

The trip back to Dawson City had passed surprisingly quickly. As Max and Brian stepped into Max's apartment, Max's phone rang again, the loud electronic melody shattering the silence like a hammer on ice. Sighing, Max looked down at it, annoyed. He really wasn't one for talking on the phone. He much preferred to text or talk face to face but apparently someone wanted to get a hold of him.

The caller ID this time wasn't unknown but was rather very much a known caller.

Raven.

He cast an apologetic look at Brian and shrugged his shoulders, showing him the ID as the phone continued to warble. Brian breathed out a sharp sigh of frustration and shook his head and moved off into the living room, carrying the box and jacket. Max, knowing he couldn't avoid it anymore, answered the call, sliding his finger over to the green **ACCEPT**.

Pulling the phone up to his ear as he tossed his truck keys on the counter with a clatter, he heard Raven's voice and he knew she was not happy.

"My God Max where have you been? I've been trying to reach you for days. Two days as a matter of fact. Are you okay? Where's Brian? Did you find out anything?"

Her words were blasting, running onto each other in her rush to express herself and Max shook his head, even though she couldn't see it.

"Hold on...hold on. Slow down. Please." He said as he walked into the living room and sat down on the couch next to Brian who gave the phone the stink eye.

Max pulled the phone away from his ear and hit the speakerphone.

"Now, we're both right here and we can both hear you."

Both of them heard Raven sigh and she started over again, slower this time, her voice sounding small and electronic coming from the phone's speaker.

Outside the apartment, Brian heard a car horn blare at the intersection and someone screamed a particularly vile obscenity at the offender. His ears jerked towards the sound unconsciously. On the phone, Raven continued.

"I'm sorry," she said. "First, are both of you okay?"

Max shrugged. "I'm fine. Same old same old. No bullet holes if that's what you're asking."

Brian thought he heard relief in Raven's voice but he wasn't too partial to care at the moment as she asked for him.

"And Brian?"

Max looked over at Brian, who had returned his attention to the call at the sound of his name..

"I'm fine, Raven." Brian said quietly.

"Why haven't you two been answering? I was worried about you." Her voice asked, and Brian snorted.

"Were you so worried about us that you asked Max to do something incredibly stupid and not tell anyone else so that if he got in over his head he'd have no back up?" Brian snarled quietly at her.

"What are you talking about?" Raven shot back, her tone suddenly unsteady.

Brian's volume instantly went up as he growled, and leaned into the speaker phone, his tone sliding fully into quiet frustrated anger. His curving incisors flashed as he replied.

"You know damn well what I'm talking about. You told Max to go out and find out where that drug is coming from and he did. He nearly died, Raven. If I hadn't followed him, he would have! You didn't tell anyone, not even me because your ass didn't trust me or anyone else to help him!"

Max tried to interject but the fire was already lit and it was burning out of control quickly.

"Brian, Max has been doing this for years. He's no fool and you're right; I didn't trust you or anyone else with this. I didn't know whether or not you could handle doing what he does. I didn't know if you could remain level headed. That drug is the reason your best friend is dead and why you are the way you are. If it hadn't been for it and the events it set in motion, you wouldn't be here!"

Her words raked at Brian like a cat scratch on the face. He wasn't gentle when he replied.

"Goddamn, Raven. That sounds like the stupidest reason I could have ever made up in my fucking life. You know very well that I'm not some loose fucking cannon. I know what I'm doing. I can fight! You had no right to hide this from me. I deserved to know that you were tracking this shit down because it put me here!"

When Raven came back she too had lost her temper.

"Brian there is more than you know going on here. We've found some things, things I suspected but couldn't verify about you. There are some things you need to know! I can't in good conscience put your life in danger when we don't know what you are capable of! I didn't want to tell you until I was sure!"

Brian flinched at that, his ears pinning to the top of his head, his green eyes blazing.

"What the hell does that even mean? I'm not some glass knick-knack you stick on your fucking shelf to study. I know it's going to be a big boost to your medical career when you finally get to publish a paper or something about me but fuck, Raven..."

"No, Brian it's not that—"

"Then what is it?"

Raven sighed on the other end and for a few seconds, the entire apartment was silent except the three of them breathing and finally she broke the silence.

"Look, we can discuss this later. Right now, I need both of you to come up to Forest Glen. We've found out some things, like I said. I may have some answers for you. Rakinos tampered with our systems and we've managed to fix them and we found what he tried to hide and Brian, this concerns you so will both of you please just come up as soon as you can?"

Her voice sounded tired and strangely, a bit scared, Brian thought. He looked at Max at the mention of Rakinos' name.

Brian just shook his head and went back to being silent. Max looked at him for a moment, frowning and then back to the phone.

"We may have something on that, too. The Rakinos bit. Give us a bit to get cleaned up. We were at Brian's mom's house last night. We found some things out on our end as well. We'll see you in a bit."

"Thank you...and... guys.... please...be careful."

"We will, Raven." Max told her.

Max ended the call with a tap of the screen and tossed the phone onto the coffee table, making the ashtray with bullets and the empty beer bottles rattle.

"Well, that was awkward as fuck. You do have a temper." Max said, though not judgmentally. When Brian met his eyes, he saw the tiniest hint of a mischievous smile there.

Brian snorted when he replied.

"Well, it takes a while and a lot to get it to come out. I try to control it." He sighed. "I spent long enough in anger management classes as a kid trying to beat it. I don't want to be that person I was again but sometimes..." he finished as his voice dropped off, letting his furry black hands fall between his knees as he gave Max a shrug. "I get defensive when it comes to people I care about."

Max reached over and put an arm around Brian's shoulder.

"I know what you mean. I'm the same way. I feel like I run from my ghosts every day. But I'm tough, man, try not to worry too much. Normally I can handle this stuff pretty well but honestly," Max said and gave him a wry warm smile. "I'm glad you're here with me. Feels good to have back up out there. I'm not used to it but it was nice."

He sighed.

"Don't let Raven get to you too much; she means well but sometimes her academic mind can outthink her heart. She does care for us. We're all a family.... just a bit dysfunctional." He said, looking at Brian with a kinder look than Brian was used to seeing from him and his normally gruff behavior.

Sighing, Brian nodded and tried to explain. "I know. I just don't like being left out of the loop. It bugs me. It's one of my red buttons; it always has been since my dad died. He did it for years and I felt like it put distance between us. I don't want that here."

Max nodded and his ears lowered a little. His eyes said all that needed to be said but he spoke anyway.

"I understand. I'll try my best to make sure it doesn't happen again." Max grinned softly. "But...we made a pretty good team...well...you did. I was an idiot and got myself knocked out but still...No more hiding things from each other."

The room fell quiet for a few moments. Suddenly, Max's eyes lit up and he ruffled Brian's fur on the top of his head, playfully.

"Hey, how about I call Ash and see about setting the two of you up together so you can ask him about a job? You said you didn't know if you were going back to the hospital. Then, I'd like to shower. Feeling a bit scummy." He finished.

"A shower sounds good. And Max? Thanks. I appreciate it." Brian added, kicking his shoes off.

Max nodded quietly, picked his arm up off of Brian. He picked up the phone again and dialed a number. Brian heard the phone ring and felt his ears twitch towards the sound. A moment later, a husky voice answered.

"Wolves Den."

"Ash, its Max."

The voice on the other end seemed to pause for a moment and then snorted.

"Yeah, what's up?"

Max looked at Brian as he spoke. "Was wondering if you had any positions at the club you needed filled? You've not met him yet but it's the same guy that Raven and I brought in a while back. He's a security guard at the hospital. The big hospital downtown. He's had a rough two weeks. Thought I'd give you a call first. He's good in a fight and sharp."

There was a pause as if the voice on the other end of the line was thinking and then a reply which made Brian's mood lift a bit.

"You know, I might have a spot open. I need a bouncer and security. Blaine's been looking for a replacement for Cody for weeks now. Need to interview him but yeah, it's a possibility. When can he come by? It would be good to have someone with experience we can count on."

Max looked at Brian who shrugged. Brian mouthed "today" and Max nodded.

"Well, we're headed out to your brother's in a bit. We could stop by before we leave the city. Bout an hour or so. Sound good?"

"Yeah sounds good. I'll tell Blaine. See you then."

The line went dead.

"Guessing he's not much of a talker either?" Brian asked as Max put the phone on the table again, gently this time.

"Well, he is, it's just that any time his brother is brought up it gets...twitchy. You might want to avoid that unless he brings it up directly."

Brian nodded his head. "What's the plan?"

"Showers then we can head out. Still pretty stuffed from your mom's."

"Sounds good."

With that, Max boosted his large frame off the couch and made towards the bathroom.

Brian sat on the couch, his mind turning in multiple directions as faces and feelings floated through the mental space in his head. The prospect of a new job and getting away from the hospital was nice. It was something new and new was good right now. It helped ease some of the apprehension he was having about learning to fit into this new culture and society of his, which he had to admit, didn't seem all that different from the one he had left behind. Granted, he admitted, that he had not gotten to experience much of shifter life outside of the chaos that had been the last two weeks and he wondered if time would change his mind.

He thought about Raven. He liked her or at least, he wanted to. She had been kind to him at first and seemed genuinely concerned about his well-being. Didn't that warrant some leeway?

Maybe, he thought settling back into the couch, listening to Max shuffle around in the bathroom, the door to the bathroom partially closed. He sniffed and could smell Max's musky scent. It wasn't bad, he thought.

He liked it.

Raven came back in his head again.

She should have told me, he thought bitterly. His rational mind kicked him in the shins for that. She didn't really know him that well as a person; they passed each other in the hallways at work and barely spoke much beyond the rare coffee break they happened to share. She cared enough about her patients to ask Max to find the source and that meant more people had been victims of that shit. He wondered absently whatever happened to the guy he and Elijah had turned over to the cops. The drug had cost him his best friend.

Then the big thought hit him. Should he forgive Raven? Forgive her for what? His mind shot back. She was right in what she did but his heart argued she wasn't. He was about to start a mental thought cycle, he could tell, like he always did when things bothered him but a sound drew his attention and made his ears swivel towards the bathroom. It was Max and there was something about his voice that was different. It was softer, more hesitant.

"Hey, Brian..."

Turning to face it, Brian called back. "Yeah?"

"Want to shower with me?"

Brian felt his eyes go large and felt his ears drop in surprise. A cold jolt ran through him but not of fear. Rather, it was just pure surprise.

What should I say, what is the right thing here? he thought desperately and before he knew what he was doing, he was on his feet, his heart talking for his brain that seemed to suddenly find itself on vacation.

"Sure." He called back as he moved across the room and paused before the bathroom door, his heart suddenly speeding up in his chest as blood rushed through his veins, making his hands shake. In fact, he felt himself begin to tremble all over as a strange warmth blossomed in his core that he recognized.

Desire. Need. Want.

Brian reached out a hand and pushed open the bathroom door and it swung wide.

He was expecting to see Max standing there or something but no, Max was already in the wide large shower, the glass door on it pulled shut, the frosted panes revealing his large frame behind it and his ears sticking up just above the top of the shower line.

"I hope you don't mind the water being too warm," Max said, sputtering a bit as water ran into his mouth.

"N-no it's fine." Brian said.

"Well, come on in." Max told him and Brian took a deep breath. He wondered why he was so nervous now. It wasn't like they hadn't been together before. The last time was different, he thought. The last time was all instinct, passion, driven by something deeper and more primal, of pent up emotion and drive. This was conscious action and thought.

Gathering his courage, reminding himself that it was just Max, he pulled his shirt off, unbuckled and dropped his pants and trunks and stood, naked. He caught a glimpse of himself in the mirror and this time, looking upon his thickly furred broad body and tail, with its wolf snout and canine head, he didn't mind it. He saw something more now than he did before. He didn't see a mystery anymore but rather, he saw something that was very much a part of him and he smiled a bit at himself, something to be proud of.

He slid open the shower door and Max stood there, beneath the running waterfall of the shower head, the water streaming down his face and shoulders, his blue eyes warm and welcoming, totally different from his normally hard exterior. He was totally drenched, his fur matted down and sleekly wet like an otter.

He extended an open hand to Brian and smiled.

"Come on in."

Brian nodded and after a second's hesitation, took it and Max pulled him into the shower, sliding the door closed behind him.

Instantly Brian felt the hot water strike him with millions of tiny light touches and in moments, he too was soaked from head to tail, his fur pushed close to his skin, and it felt wonderful as the heat loosened up his muscles and relaxed the tension he was feeling from the brief bitter argument with Raven. He closed his eyes and breathed in and out slowly, letting his chest rise and fall, his tail falling still behind him, basking in the heat and the welcome humidity.

When he opened his eyes, Max had moved in closer. They were now standing inches apart from each other as the water cascaded down around them both. They were practically nose to nose and blue eyes stared into green eyes.

"Hey there..." Brian said huskily, his voice quiet and thicker than usual.

"Hey." Max replied gently and leaned in, his nose touching Brian's. For a time, it felt like hours, they stood like that, the water drowning them together, dark and darker, blending together as seamlessly as the night sky.

Brian leaned in and a moment later, he and Max were locked in a kiss that was long, deep and had nothing of the primal drive from the last time but this time something far more powerful, far deeper and far reaching in its scope and meaning. Brian reached up and put one hand around the back of Max's head and the other on his waist. Max's arms found their way around Brian's body and they let the outside world go. In this moment, the world had no place, no meaning; here there was only solace, silence and peace. There was no screaming, no bullets, no fighting. No lies, no shadows, only warmth and light. There was no snowstorm, no ghosts and no dream monsters.

When they finally broke apart, each nestled into the others neck.

"This is the most powerful thing I think I've ever felt...and I'm scared of it." Max whispered into Brian's shoulder and neck.

Brian could feel the bigger werewolf tremble.

Brian nodded. "I'm scared too..."

He felt Max nod. "I don't know how to fight it. I don't know how to deal with it. It's wonderful but I feel like I'm flailing in my head...."

Brian pulled back and held Max's head with one hand gently laid up on the side of his cheek.

"I know. I've only felt this one other time and... well...you know how that went. I'm not scared of feeling...I'm scared of losing it again." he told Max honestly.

Max frowned slightly and laid his head back onto Brian's shoulder. He spoke quietly, water dripping from his chin.

"I've been looking for this kind of peace for a long time...I never thought it would be you that I would find it in but I can promise you this if you promise me the same..."

Brian nodded. "What's that?"

"That if we do this for real, that if we commit, that we'll always have each other's back and always come home to each other. I can't lose another family. I can't lose someone I love again." Max finished.

Brian felt like he was stabbed in the heart but not because of Max's words but the meaning behind them. The context. That was the true heart of Max's problems, his nightmares, his quest.

The fear of being alone. Abandoned.

Brian pulled his head back and looked deep into Max's eyes.

"You'll never lose me because I won't let that happen. I'll always be there. No matter what."

He felt Max nod and Brian put his arms around him and held him tightly. He wondered if some day, he would be strong enough to push the pieces of Max back together again and hoped he was up to the task.

After a few moments, the two of them stood apart and Max sniffed a bit before his normal self returned and he made a snorting sound.

"So, uh, we should get washed up...."

Brian grinned "Yeah, we should."

Max reached onto the shower caddy and grabbed a bottle of Bearglove shower gel, the kind that was specially conditioned for shifter's fur.

"What, no Wolfthorn?"

"I ran out." Max chuckled.

He squirted a big green-blue blob of it into his hands and motioned Brian to come closer.

"I'm not helpless," Brian said with a laugh.

Max shrugged and grinned. "Doesn't matter. Come here, pup."

Doing as he was told, Brian felt Max's large hands work their way over him, digging deeply into his fur, down to his undercoat, brushing the skin, going in deep circles. Starting at his neck and moving down to his shoulders, Max worked the shower gel into his arms, sliding over to his chest and stomach. It felt like the best damn massage he had ever gotten. In fact, Brian thought, it had nearly lulled him into being jelly legged. Max's fingers passed over his nipples and he felt a surge of excitement run through him and resisted it as Max worked down lower, passing through the ridges of his stomach muscles, circling closer and lower to the hard V of his groin.

"Here... let me help you..." Brian said and grabbed the gel and after squirting a glob of it into his hands, lathered them up and began to work Max over the same way, moving the same way, trying to imitate what Max had done.

Within a short span of time, both of them were covered in thick white sudsy lather that smelled amazing and masculine, clean and sharp. Brian gasped as Max moved between his legs, gently scrubbing the inside of his thighs parting the fur there, sliding over his penis and gently cupping his scrotum, being extra careful not to hurt him.

"That feels pretty good," Brian commented, his face flushing hot as Max looked up at him.

"Gotta get it all clean you know..." he replied with the tiniest of evil grins. He slid Brian's foreskin back and washed carefully there, sending waves of pleasure down Brian's spine.

"If I didn't know any better, I'd say that you're doing that on purpose." Brian told him as he worked his hands and fingers deep into the thick fur of Max's neck and undercoat.

Max simply shrugged innocently and came back up and began scrubbing Brian's neck again and behind his ears, working his way into the ears themselves. That tickled and Brian laughed, getting soap in his mouth. He spat it out and he heard a sound he hadn't really heard before and he had to do a double take.

It was a rich sound, deep and genuine with a slight bass to it.

It was a sound of happiness and amusement and he recognized what it was immediately.

Max was laughing at him. Real, genuine laugher.

Brian stopped washing Max's chest and looked up at him with one eye cracked open.

"Did you just laugh at me?" he asked as his own soaked fur hung in his eyes. He blew it out of his face.

Max nodded, still chuckling. "I think I did."

Brian felt something explode within himself like a hot firework. It was a great feeling. It swelled inside of him and he grinned like an idiot from ear to perky ear.

"It's about time." He said gently and wiped the soap away from Max's cheeks and snout.

Max simply nodded, grinning like an idiot, the water falling around them like rain. Brian put his arms around Max and pulled him into an embrace. Max returned it, and this time, there was nothing but warmth and he finally felt the connection he had been longing for, finally found the peace he needed.

An electronic melody began to play and Max's ears perked towards it. The phone was ringing again. Brian looked from Max, through the glass of the shower and then out the bathroom door towards the living room.

"Let it ring...this is our time..." Max said his voice husky and he closed the space with Brian again and Brian felt Max's lips on his and surrendered to him as he found himself up against the wall of the shower, the slick wet tile pressing against his back as Max's erection pushed against his own.

In minutes, the two of them were lost in a storm of each other, the water cascading around them, washing the suds away as they met and became one again, taking turns with each other, loving and needing all at once, going much further this time, fully exploring. Their gentle grunts and growls were lost to the sound of the shower and for the next half an hour, neither of them had a single thought except of the other.

Out in the living room, the phone continued to ring before finally stopping, its screen flashing *MISSED CALL*.

The caller ID read simply *UNKNOWN CALLER* as the phone screen went dark.

There was no voicemail as steam from the bathroom wafted into the living room like ghosts finally leaving their old haunt behind.

CHAPTER 3

"So, what makes you want to be here, aside from the amazing company and atmosphere?" the grey furred werewolf with black tiger stripes asked sardonically as he leaned back into a chair at a table in The Wolves Den. This fellow, Brian had learned, was Ash Riley, the guy Max had mentioned, the club owner and brother to Draco Riley.

He was shorter than Brian, standing just barely six foot three and was probably three hundred pounds of muscle. He was wearing a clean white polo shirt with the club logo on it in black silhouette on the right breast and a pair of neat jeans and shoes with his shirt tucked in. The black stripes on his fur stood out in stark contrast to the lighter colors of the rest of him. Both of his ears were pierced at least twice with small simple silver rings and there was also a bull ring that hung from his nose as well, nothing too huge but it was there nonetheless, in stainless steel.

The grey werewolf's voice was pure Dawson City: tough, no nonsense with a healthy dose of sarcasm. He also had his brother's ocean blue-green eyes and the fur under his chin and jaw line was darker than the rest of his fur, a dark blackish brown, forming a thin but neat beard.

This is the DJ that was on the stage the first night I was here, Brian thought as he looked at him, *only now he has a shirt on and looks like a business man instead of a rocker. If it wasn't for the stripes and piercings, I'd probably not know it was the same guy. He's got a totally different demeanor.*

Around them, the club itself was nearly empty, the dance floor deserted, the warm afternoon sunlight filtering down through the darkly tinted windows. The bar had a few regulars but otherwise, it was a quiet afternoon. Soft music played over the speakers, and it sounded familiar but Brian couldn't place it. The two of them sat a round table near the very same one in the bar area that Brian had his first meal as a shifter. Max had wandered off to give them some privacy and as he glanced up, Max was talking to another shifter.

Brian swung his attention back to the interview.

"All of my life, I tried to live up to my dad's ideals and recently I found out he wasn't the man I thought he was; he was something more. I want to learn about this part of his life, this part of our culture, society, to find a spot where I belong. He was a werewolf, like me, but I didn't know that until recently."

Nodding, Ash looked Brian over again. The young werewolf in front of him was cleanly and simply dressed. He wore a dark navy-blue shirt and jeans; he'd even tucked his shirt in, Ash thought, amused. Around his neck he wore a thin silver chain upon which a richly engraved Celtic ring hung. He was black furred with strange green eyes and a silver blaze that peeked out over his shirt collar and extended up his neck a little.

When he spoke next, Ash's voice turned more serious.

"I know who you are, at least on the surface. Raven told me about you. I was the one who told her you could use the facilities downstairs. You are one hell of a puzzle and you've got all kinds of people talking. Well, in my brother's circle anyway. I try to steer clear of that."

Brian saw a look flash over Ash's face and Brian thought he may have understood what it meant, given what Draco had told him. Given that history, he thought it would be a wise idea to keep his mouth shut, knowing what he did about Ash's sister and the disharmony between the brothers.

Ash continued, putting his hands on the table as he leaned in.

"So, you're a guard up at Wade Johnson. That's not too bad. They train you guys well from what I hear. What I'm looking for is someone who not only provides security but also enforces it, someone with brains and brawn but who knows what it means to be a goddamn professional, not a thug." Ash said, pinning Brian with an analyzing gaze. "Sometimes we get drug runners in here, trouble makers. I need someone who can investigate and eliminate the problem before anyone gets hurt. I don't want that trouble in my club for a lot of reasons."

Brian shrugged. "I've handled everything from bed rails to bed pans being thrown in my face; I've been slashed, spat on and called everything in the book."

"I bet you have. Max speaks well about you too. That means something in my book. I may try to stay out of the politics but Max is a good guy. If he says I can trust you I can. I'd like you to meet my chief of security and let him talk to you to see what he thinks. The last guy Cody, well, he was a handful. He lasted a lot longer than he should have. If Blaine thinks you've got what we need, I'll bring you on."

Brian nodded, feeling his heart slow down a bit. He hadn't known what to expect from Ash Riley or this job interview. It had gone on for over an hour as Ash grilled him about his past jobs, his experience, his training and even how he knew Max. Brian was grateful that he had told the truth since apparently Ash already knew more about him than Brian would normally like. Given his connection to Draco, however, it didn't bother Brian as much as it normally would.

"Hey, Blaine!" Ash called out, looking over his shoulder as he half turned in his chair.

Across the room, the shifter that Max had been talking to perked his ears up and turned to face them.

"Yeah?" the shifter called back.

"Come here, if you don't mind. I need you for a moment." Ash told him.

Brian felt his eyes go wide as Blaine came closer and he realized just how massive the guy actually was, and now that he was closer and in the light Brian realized that he was in fact the same giant dark furred shifter guard that he had seen at the club standing on the platform with the eerie glowing blue eyes.

The man resembled a Rottweiler with some Akita thrown in, though in terms of color, he was pure Rottweiler, jet black with rich tan fur on his hands that went a little bit past his wrists. A fluffy black and brown tail curled behind him and his ears stood at attention while his eyes were a rich chocolate brown. There was something odd about his ears, but Brian couldn't quite place it. They weren't exactly like a Rottweiler but stouter and more triangular, standing up. Blaine's face and muzzle were heavy and wide, his jaws were heavily muscled. In fact, man was a walking bulldozer made of muscle. He towered over Max at six foot eight at the least and probably outweighed both him and Max easily; Brian estimated he had to be close to five hundred pounds of raw power, and his build reminded Brian of power lifters he had seen in strongman competitions. His black polo work shirt with the club logo in white on the right breast was stretched tightly across his broad chest and thick solid torso and his khaki pants were the same. Filled.

He seemed like he was going to burst out of them and Brian swallowed, suddenly nervous. *The guy could probably break me in two*, he thought. Blaine's thick dark brown eyebrows on his black and tan face rose a bit when he saw Brian but he said nothing at first, his gentle brown eyes studying the younger shifter carefully. They had none of the eerie blue night-shine they had before. His thick brown beard was neatly kept and framed his canine face well. The brown blaze on his chest poked out over his shirt collar.

"Brian, this is Blaine Yukon, my chief of security. He's been with me a long time, and I trust him with my life. He's also a good friend of mine so I listen to him. Blaine, this is Brian, the guy I told you about who's trying to find a job in security."

Blaine stuck out a massive meaty hand with thick fingers and Brian reached up and took it. His hand vanished into the black and tanned shifter's appendage but he gave it a solid shake, nonetheless. It felt pathetic.

After letting go of Brian's hand, Blaine seemed to size him up.

"So, you've got security training. What else you got, shorty?" Blaine asked, not condescendingly but just easily, which didn't really match his exterior. Brian was expecting gruff and mean, not relaxed and at ease. A warm grin revealed Blaine's pearly white incisors.

Recovering his ability to speak and reminding himself mentally that he was not short at six foot four, Brian replied.

"Er, uh, well, I got the basic passive nonviolent restraint training. Some boxing and two years of kendo. Some tae-kwon do as well."

"Kendo, huh? That's actually impressive. Any weapon specialty?"

Brian shook his head. "Not really. I only took it for two years after my dad died. I didn't get far but maybe if I had to say any one in particular it would be a staff. I seem to have a knack for it."

Blaine nodded and snorted approvingly, still wearing that warm grin.

"Come show me what you got. Dance floor is clear. Want to see if you can back up what you say you can."

Brian blanched under his fur. "Here? Now?"

Blaine raised one of his brown eyebrows. "Where else would be better?"

Nodding, Brian realized that Blaine did have a valid point.

Ash stood up and looked at them. "While you two are doing that, I'll be right back. Call of nature. MacGregor, Blaine is no push over." With that, he scooted his chair back and made his way back towards the bathrooms, leaving Max to watch, trusting Blaine to give Brian a fair evaluation.

As Ash passed Blaine, he gave the bigger werewolf a raised eyebrow and Blaine just smirked back at him wordlessly. Ash chuckled and shook his head, leaving Blaine to take over.

The low music over the speakers filled the sudden silence of Ash's absence.

"Come on, then. No time like the present!" Blaine barked, an almost cocky grin spreading over his tan muzzle.

Brian swallowed as he got up out of the seat and followed the hulking werewolf back over to the dance floor which, as Blaine had said, was empty and free of people. It was also spotlessly clean. As he got up, of the corner of his eye, he saw Max pick up and turn his chair around so he could sit, facing the two of them. Brian reminded himself to not be nervous but for some reason, having Max watching him made that extremely difficult.

Once they arrived on the dance floor, Blaine took up a position to the left and Brian made to go to the right.

"I'm not going to say what I'm going to do, and that's how it's going to be in real life a bar fight. I'm a lot bigger than you, and that happens sometimes, too. People fight dirty. You get dirty. Let's roll, short stuff."

Brian didn't know what to expect from the big shifter so when Blaine dropped into a fighting stance, Brian did the same and it began.

They circled each other like alpha animals, round and round, each one assessing the other. Brian looked for weak points, favored feet or limbs and found nothing. He thought he could use the giant shifter's size to his advantage but if he failed or Blaine turned it against him, he'd end up with his face smashed into the concrete floor.

While Brian was analyzing, Blaine choose that moment to move in.

The speed with which he moved was unreal and caught Brian totally unprepared. Brian was expecting from Blaine's almost waddling walk for him to be slower but no, he instantly became a black and tan streak, a streak that slammed into Brian with a powerful shoulder ram, sending Brian tumbling backward on his ass.

With a yelp of surprise, the concrete floor smacked into him and Brian rolled quickly knowing now what he was up against and knowing that there would be no quarter.

He came up to his feet using the momentum of his fall to propel himself back up.

Blaine grinned as he turned and faced the younger shifter.

"You got back up. Not bad. Not many people can take a hit like that and stand up. Color me impressed, short stuff."

Blaine moved again, closing the distance between the two of them, taking shots at Brian's ribs, his legs and lastly his face, his tan fists and thick black forearms becoming powerful blurs.

Brian struggled to repel the blows, grunting with the effort it took to hold back the much bigger werewolf. It was like fighting a freight train. Brian actually felt beads of sweat pop on his forehead but he blocked each and every one, barely, his forearms rattling with the force of the impacts, his heart thudding in his chest.

Blaine rained down another blow which Brian blocked, trapping the bigger werewolf's fist between his own arms in an arm lock. Blaine pulled against him and Brian put all the strength he could muster into it, the muscles in his forearms and biceps bulging with the effort. Blaine looked like he was barely trying at all.

"Nice arm lock, let me show you how to beat it." He grinned.

Blaine pushed into the arm lock rather than tried to pull away and that forced Brian backward, and with the sudden change in momentum, he found his grip on Blaine's arm failing. Blaine took the chance and sent Brian across the dance floor.

Brian crashed hard into the concrete floor, sending up a bit of dust as he landed, driving the wind out of him and for a moment he saw stars. He groaned in pain and tried to stand up. He saw Blaine come at him and with a growl of effort, Brian forced himself to leap back to his feet, his tail lashing behind him as his ears pinned down against his head. He could feel his own temper rising. He knew this was simply a test but damn. There was no need to show him up for it.

It's your own fault for being weak and foolish, not his. His mind snapped at him out of nowhere and with a snarl of anger that was quite unusual for him, Brian charged Blaine, determined to knock the big werewolf onto his black and tan ass.

Seeing Brian's mistake, Blaine easily took advantage of it and simply caught Brian's thrown right hook and swirled him into a painful arm bar, locking him in place, halting his momentum instantly. Brian felt the searing heat shoot up his shoulder as

Blaine forced the lock harder, bending Brian over closer to the floor. Brian couldn't break the lock without breaking his arm. Blaine's body was pressed up against his and he could feel the heat of it coming through his shirt.

"Your temper may get you killed. You need to watch that. It's a rookie mistake. You should know that. Calm down and think when you fight." Blaine said, grunting through clenched teeth as Brian struggled, his breath warm on the back of Brian's neck.

He didn't let Brian's arm go.

"Think it through. How do you get out of an armbar when the someone is bigger, stronger, and meaner than you? What you do could get you killed. You need to think fast and think right!" Blaine growled with effort.

Brian could feel the larger shifter's weight on him, the sharp clean scent of his cologne.

He felt something stir inside him and then the little voice in his head was back, the same growling snarling presence from his dreams again. It was the shadowy monster that lurked in his mind and he felt it coming out like a bad dream, crawling in his skull.

Brian struggled to get loose and tell Blaine to back off, for a just a moment. That something was wrong but he couldn't. The arm bar was too painful. His heart hammered in his chest and his temper edged into the red. He was failing, and he didn't like failing. He was trapped, like a rat, and a deep instinctual panic set in as his adrenaline began to flow into the sea of claustrophobia that was suddenly draping over him.

His pulse began to race.

Brian's eyes flared white.

No one saw his eyes change.

With a deadly quiet snarl that vibrated his chest, he stood up, taking Blaine's full weight as if it was nothing. He shoved upwards and used that momentum to swing around, becoming a black blur as he did. He reversed the arm bar and used Blaine's own weight to lift him over his shoulder and slam the bigger werewolf to the ground in a single violent body slam.

Blaine landed hard, the sound muffled from the music, the breath driven from him with a yelp of surprise more than pain as Brian stood over him, panting, his eyes blazing white, holding Blaine's arm in a lock that would have torn it from the socket had Blaine tried to move. Blaine tried to get free but struggled in vain.

Across the room, Max stood up, crossing over to the two of them and a bolt of fear shot through him as Brian, hearing Max as he come closer, turned to face him.

His eyes...his eyes.... what the hell... Max thought, as an imaginary hand gripped his chest and squeezed.

Brian's eyes had turned silver white and were burning like hot white suns with no iris, no pupil. In the shadows that crossed Brian's face, Max saw something else, a primal animalistic rage, raw power waiting to be unleashed. Whatever was taking over Brian wasn't the same laid back generally quiet fellow he had grown to know. This was someone, no, something else entirely. Brian turned back to Blaine and raised his free hand into a clawed fist, fully intending to drive it through Blaine' skull.

If I don't do something, he's going to kill Blaine...

Max leaped forward and grabbed Brian's wrist, halting the blow he was going to drop on Blaine's face. Max struggled. Brian was suddenly stronger than he remembered. It was like trying to hold back a semi-truck. Snarling, baring his fangs, Brian turned on Max. Max leaned in, getting right in Brian's face before sharply calling his name again in a quiet but deadly serious whisper.

"Brian!"

Hearing his name come from Max as he looked in his eyes, Brian stopped cold. The blazing white eyes showed a slow recognition of Max as Max maintained his hold on Brian's arm.

Brian's growl slowed and grew quieter.

Blaine was on the ground writhing but smartly had stopped trying to get out of the lock, his eyes closed in agony as Brian's raw power stretched the muscles in his arm to the breaking point. The bigger werewolf gritted his teeth but he was essentially helpless.

A second later, a look of confusion crossed Brian's face as he looked from Max to Blaine and back. The look turned into a grimace and a moment later, the angry shadow that was swimming over Brian's face melted away as he closed his eyes and shook his head, as if he was dazed.

When he opened them, his green eyes had returned, his gaze slow and almost drugged, like he was just waking up from a dream.

Looking down, Brian saw that Blaine was quite incapacitated and quickly let him go, standing back looking down at his black furred hands in shock, confusion and fear. Max frowned. Something wasn't right. It was as if Brian had no idea where he was or what had happened.

"Wh... what..." he muttered in confusion.

With a grunt, Blaine pulled himself up off the ground and approached a stunned and quiet Brian, rubbing his burly but now very sore shoulder. He gave the smaller werewolf a smirk.

"Damn boy. I've been around a long time and I've not seen anything like that, well ever. I don't know how you got out of that arm bar but fuck me you got one hell of a set of moves on you. You tossed me like a sack of grain! I'd be happy to have you if you want the job. You might be able to teach me a thing or two!"

He said this while grinning a bit, slapping Brian on the shoulder good naturedly. He had apparently enjoyed the rough and tumble fight but Max looked at Brian whose eyes were full of fear. Both of their backs were turned as Ash returned from the bathroom and a look of surprise crossed the striped shifter's snout as he saw Blaine limping away and rubbing his arm.

"What happened to you? Did he actually win?" Ash smirked as Blaine pulled him aside excitedly and the two began to talk between themselves, leaving Max and Brian alone.

Max closed the distance between them protectively, shielding Brian from Ash's view while Ash and Blaine talked. Max quickly verified they weren't looking and turned his attention back to Brian with a glance at Blaine, wondering if the big werewolf knew just how close he had come to being seriously hurt.

"Max... what happened? I don't remember how Blaine got on the floor...I..." Brian asked, his voice shaky and quiet, afraid.

Max looked him over quickly and he replied quietly his gruff voice barely over a whisper.

"I don't know. I've never seen anything like that. Are you okay? Your eyes...they turned white...like no iris or pupils...like comic book white. Your face...it changed...became darker and it's like your whole personality did a 180. I thought you were going to kill Blaine. He's never lost a fight or a sparring match that I can remember...You threw him like he was nothing." Max told him in a quiet rush.

Brian looked from Max to Blaine, who was apparently oblivious to the danger he had just escaped and was laughing and talking animatedly about the sparring match with Ash, catching him up on what he had missed.

Brian felt a cold fear run down his spine like someone had poured ice water down the back of his shirt as he looked at his hands and then back up at Max.

"Max, I remember Blaine putting me in an arm bar and then I got angry and then nothing. It's like something else took over." He said, looking down at his own hands again, his voice trembling.

In his mind, flashes of the warehouse fight blossomed in shades of black and white streaked with scarlet red. He remembered being held down by those thugs and then.... then he remembered simply standing in front of Max who was barely conscious and being surrounded by bodies, most them in agony, barely breathing and others, very much not breathing.

Flashes shot through his mind of a giant hulking wolflike beast with black claws and teeth, with burning white eyes.

He heard the ghostly echo of a snarl and the distant sounds of claws raking flesh.

Missing time. It had happened again. The first time was the warehouse fight and now here, again..

Brian swallowed and looked up at Max. Dark realization sunk in.

"Max I think something *is* wrong with me.... I think I killed those people in the warehouse...at least some of them. But I don't remember doing it. Something happened..."

Max frowned. "Not that I'm complaining but what do you mean? I was out of it. I didn't see anything. I woke up and you were standing there trying to get me up. I thought you fought them off?"

Brian shook his head. "No. I tried. They grabbed me and I was pretty much dead to rights, then something happened. I don't remember anything until I was standing over you... I've got gaps in my memory and this is the second time now. I think Raven was right about me. Something's wrong."

Max frowned and considered.

"She said she found something, something Rakinos tried to hide. I meant to tell you before but we got sidetracked. I think we should get you to Forest Glen now so she can look you over, especially if you're starting to have memory gaps."

Max said and quickly acted normal as both Ash and Blaine approached.

Brian did his best to look winded, shoving his shaking hands into his jeans pockets and tried not to look terrified out of his mind and apparently it worked because neither Blaine nor Ash seemed to notice anything was out of the ordinary. Blaine was already walking better and he seemed over all none the worse for wear. If anything, he looked excited and happy.

Ash looked from Blaine to Brian and shrugged. He stuck out his hand.

"Well, I like you and Blaine thinks you've got what it takes. The job is yours if you want it, man. If you can put this bulldozer on his ass, then, damn, you can handle anything the club might throw at you." Ash said and held out his hand. Swallowing, Brian reached out and took it, shaking it slowly.

"Yeah...I'd like that." he managed to get out.

"Come by next Friday at 8PM. We'll get you set up!" Ash called as he turned and headed upstairs to where the office presumably was. Blaine looked at Brian.

"For a smaller fella, lawsey, you pack a punch."

Brian didn't know what to say and stood there trying to make his mouth work.

Max forced a smile, shooting a quick glance at Brian and stepped in helpfully.

"Yeah, he does. He's full of surprises."

Blaine turned to Brian and put a meaty hand on his shoulder.

"Don't take nothing that happened here personal, now see? I like to make sure my crew knows what they're getting into. Werewolf bar fights can get nasty, since most of em are stronger than humans and some have nastier temperaments when drunk. You did good, kid. I'm impressed. I haven't been put on the floor like that in a long time. It was a good reminder that I need to keep up my own game. Don't worry about my arm; I've had worse. I'll see you Friday night next week!!"

With a final good-natured slap on the shoulder, this time more gently with a solid squeeze at the end, Blaine turned to follow Ash, leaving a very shaken Brian and Max alone.

"Let's get out of here. I... I don't feel very good." Brian said and he turned not waiting for Max as he made for the exit. Max followed him and put an arm around his shoulder reassuringly, and together, they walked out into the afternoon sun. A few moments later, they were in Max's truck and headed up the highway to Forest Glen, neither one quite knowing what to say, both afraid for very different reasons. For a while, they both road in silence that was almost unbearable and finally, with a sigh, Max broke it.

He glanced over at Brian and with his ears back, his voice low and a little unsteady, said:

"Uh...let's stop for coffee before we head up. There's a spot not far from the exit ramp that's not bad. How's that sound? I think we could both use a break to get our bearings."

Brian nodded, barely aware, his mind far away from the truck.

"Yeah...that sounds good."

In the center console between the seats, Max's phone screen lit up as it was on silent mode.

The caller ID read *UNKNOWN CALLER.*

Neither of them noticed it as the screen was turned face down and both were deep in thoughts of their own, with neither knowing what to do about anything. Max cast worried glances at Brian every few minutes unsure of how to help him, and Brian was lost in his own mind, looking at his own hands as ghostly snarls and roars played through his brain with silent echoing screams and drops flying of red scarlet blood.

#####

John Carrey stood over the shoulders of the three shifters who were themselves hunched over a bank of computers. They were completely absorbed in their work, and John's looming presence seemed to be an afterthought for them. His blue-black fur made him look like liquid black light as he moved, pacing slowly. His eyes blazed yellow in the dim blue light cast from the computer screens. He had been down here working with the tech team pinging Max Mullen's cell phone, tracking his location every few hours and confirming it with placed calls. So far, his movements made no pattern and no sense at all.

First, he had tracked him leaving Carsonville. *What the hell was in Carsonville?* John felt a part of him stir, a cautious wary part. He thought back to Lupine Freedom's operation in Carsonville over a decade ago. They had to shutter it after a sting operation nearly blew their entire cover. A nosy cop had gotten involved and someone had leaked. That leak was promptly stopped and John wondered if Max's presence in Carsonville anything had to do with that old operation. John preferred not to think about that time of his life; even now, he was torn and conflicted over it. This whole business was starting to drag up long buried feelings and he didn't like it.

He glanced at the screen of one of the workers, a brindle colored lycanthrope with close cropped ears and amber eyes. On the screen he saw reams of numbers and GPS tracking telemetry. The smaller shifter seemed to jump a bit when he finally noticed he was being watched and he looked nervously at John.

"Back to work; no issues." John told him flatly and without room for any other interpretation. The shifter instantly returned his attention to his computer.

John had other thoughts on his mind as well.

Rakinos was becoming more daring lately. The first few signs of his increased bravado was the attack on the meeting at the Library of Congress. That had taken them weeks to plan out, and he and Rakinos had had words over it due to Rakinos using it as a test bed for one of his fucking experiments. It had also strained their finances as well, having to buy off certain members of the capitol hill police force and the Secret Service who were sympathetic to the cause of Lupine Freedom. The intention behind the attack to was to remind the cowards drafting that legislation that shifters would not allow themselves to be turned into victims the same way the Japanese did in World War 2. There would be no quarter given.

At least, that was one part of the plan.

The other part of the plan was to intentionally sow chaos and to do that, Rakinos himself had secretly been pushing the registration bill with the help of a corrupt legislator. John had never been allowed to meet the guy and he didn't even know his name.

Another example of Rakinos' increasingly insular behavior, of shutting me out, John thought darkly. It was hard to put into words the conflict that was raging within him. Bringing in politicians was the last thing John had ever wanted when he first joined up. He disliked them. Immensely. *I don't trust politicians, but Rakinos trusts this one and that's all that matters anymore,* John thought frustrated. Rakinos was listening to John less and less, and John didn't care for that. John also didn't care for the experimentation using shifters. Rakinos told him they were volunteers but something about that was rubbing his fur the wrong way.

In short, he thought as he let his mind wander, Rakinos and Lupine Freedom were playing both sides, humans and werewolves, against each other: Creating the division and then working the division. A city divided was easier to break. Scared people, angry people were easy to control when they didn't think about what they were doing or being asked to do, when an authority figure told them it was okay.

It was a master stroke and a far cry from their early days as drug and gun runners. John suspected that Rakinos had actually been planning this far longer than the last few years.

When Madison had come onboard, thanks to some nudging from Kajal and her machinations, however, John thought angrily, things had changed.

Rakinos slowly became more secretive, no longer confiding in John and his entire focus had shifted into reviving and improving that damned drug. When Rakinos told him his plan for it, John had been dubious, almost outraged. Apparently, during World War 2 the Nazi SS had a division that came to call themselves the *Werwolfs*. The plan was formulated in 1944 and was the brainchild of the notorious Heinrich Himmler. The idea was to create and train an elite group of SS operatives to go behind enemy lines. Sniping, bombings, assassinations, arson. These were the tools these operatives used. To the public, the German *Werwolf* troops weren't effective but in truth, they were decimating Allied forces because some of the operatives legitimately were real werewolves, shape-shifters loyal to the Fatherland, operating in secret behind enemy lines.

Allied Commandos became desperate and with the war entering its final years, the US military decided to fight fire with fire and hand-picked elite werewolves from Allied commando units and with them, formed their own werewolf squads. These men, all supposedly volunteers, were subjected to tests, experimentations and more, all in the hopes to create a super weapon but these attempts failed but eventually the specialized commandos were deployed regardless and did reasonably well.

The Dog Soldiers, as they became known, John thought.

The drugs they used then, the methods, they were all crude, lacking a better understanding of genetics and re-sequencing, lacking the knowledge of how the brain worked. That all changed as technology began to improve. Madison and his company had somehow acquired the research and was working on it but failing miserably until Rakinos found him and together, the two of them were able to make the serums work and eventually improved it into its modern form: Wolf's Bane.

John wasn't sure what to make of the project that Rakinos was now working on. For the last few years or so, Rakinos and Madison had been an uneasy pairing, often fighting and yelling at each other for hours in frustration as they seemed to finally hit a brick wall with their wonder serum. For one, John thought, Rakinos had said the drug was too dangerous. Too potent but it had to be potent in order to stand up to the immune system of a shifter. The problem was its enhancing effects and its hypnotic byproducts burned out a shifters immune system. With the addition of a stable radioactive isotope, that problem had been mostly corrected because the radiation suppressed the immune system but without the immune system, the shifter who used it in the doses required to get the best results would die in a matter of hours, creating a short lived and quite useless super weapon.

That problem remained a continual source of stress until this whole business with this Brian MacGregor showed up. Apparently, his unique DNA had provided a means to stabilize the drug's reaction.

MacGregor.

That name had struck a chord with John and after some digging, he found out why.

Jacob MacGregor had been the lead officer in the sting years ago that nearly shook their operation apart. John remembered coming to Rakinos once he had discovered the truth. How ironic that MacGregor's son would turn out to be the final piece of the puzzle through random chance. MacGregor had only gotten involved in their plans because he was unfortunate enough to bust a drug lackey that had been selling off Lupine Freedom's stolen product, and well, now two and a half weeks later, with a few blood samples, Rakinos had found his solution.

John growled to himself. Jacob MacGregor was a memory he'd prefer to leave buried and now knowing they were going after his son years later, was troublesome.

Madison was no longer a roadblock to Rakinos either. John remembered hearing his screams as he walked through the hallways that serviced the little used prison cells. Now, Rakinos was unfettered, unleashed as it were.

Still, even with a solution to the stabilization problem found, John was wary of the idea of turning shifters into these dog soldiers. Once they were injected with the drug and DNA combo, it seemed to turn them into walking locomotives, violent beyond reason, unthinking killing machines, at least in John's opinion. He was hoping that this entire plan wasn't going to backfire, especially after at least twenty of the humans from the docks had just shown up last night and nearly caused a shootout in the exterior courtyard. The humans had surrendered immediately. He didn't know what to expect after meeting with them and now that they were here, he was even more on edge. Volunteers or not, he didn't like idea. Not one bit.

Currently, all twenty-two of them were down in the big lab off the production room floor. All of them were currently in medically induced comas as Kajal and the other scientists on the team slowly acclimated their bodies to larger and larger doses of Wolf's Bane while at the same time using a new method of subliminal narcoleptic flash training. They wouldn't be ready to be changed for a while yet.

Rakinos had used the last of unique enzyme in MacGregor's samples to turn at least four shifter volunteers and Madison as a test. At least, Rakinos told John they were volunteers, and John had no evidence to the contrary. Madison was the final test subject, to verify it would work on baseline humans. So far, he wasn't dead. The first shifter, however, the prototype, as Rakinos called him, had those strange mismatched eyes, one blue and one yellow. Something about that stirred John's memory, but he couldn't place it. Something about him was familiar but whoever he had been, that was lost now. John mentally kicked himself. He was responsible for the men under his watch. The fact that he couldn't place those eyes with a name was eating at him. Now, he mused darkly, whatever his name had been, he was something more and humanity no longer existed behind those haunted eyes.

Five people, he thought bitterly, *are now living science labs*.

The thought disturbed him deeply.

The problem was that now that Rakinos had used all the sample up; he needed a fresh DNA supply. He needed to bring MacGregor here before he could complete the process of turning the rest of the new humans into Dog Soldiers; Rakinos was already talking about modifications and improvements. The prototype, the shifter who had gotten the purest dose, seemed stable enough to make Rakinos confident that the purer the DNA, the better the result. He talked about them like software versions instead of loyal soldiers who had given their identity for their cause, and the disconnected way it was said bothered John too. There was something inherently wrong with it.

John was simply not a fan of drugs either. He had his own reasons, dark ones, and he had joined Lupine Freedom years ago to make a difference, to fight for his people so that what happened to him wouldn't happen to other shifters. For a long time, everything Rakinos had done had seemed to be just for that but lately things had changed. They had changed a lot and John wasn't a fan of the direction they were going. Not one bit.

John trusted Rakinos because Rakinos had found him in at his lowest point, and he had brought him under his wing, personally teaching him to channel his rage and anger into something productive; shaped him, formed him into a disciplined soldier. Rakinos seemed to care for him, like a son, which is why John had spent the last two days in this cramped hot tech room without complaint, directing the techs to track Mullen and presumably, Brian MacGregor, since lately the two of them seemed inseparable. He had spent years alongside Rakinos ever since the days in the fight ring and in return, Rakinos had given John a purpose, more than throwing his fists for profit and up until lately, John hadn't ever thought any other way about his leader.

But sometimes, he thought, *things change. I didn't sign up to run experiments on our own people.* Even Madison he had to admit to himself, though he was loathe to admit it.

He quietly growled at the growing conflict within himself. John despised long drawn out games even though he could appreciate the need for them. But this game, experimenting on people and tracking Mullen and MacGregor, was nearly at an end. Rakinos had told him not to engage, simply to track and so he did. For now. His loyalty was ingrained deeply but every time he looked at those malformed looking beasts, he found an uneasy questioning rising in his gut, one that caused alarm bells to go off in his mind. He just wanted this mess done with so they could go back to what Lupine Freedom meant to him.

John would have rather been out on the streets, going after the human trash that preyed on weaker werewolves. His hand unconsciously moved towards his side with the brand scar. He felt it through his fur, raised and ridged. He wondered why it never healed and vanished but in way he was glad for it. Kajal tried to explain to him why but he didn't care much for her sciences. Every day it gave him a new source of raw strength to remind him what he had come to fight against and lately, a distant part of himself thought, that hate and anger and dissatisfaction was beginning to apply to more than just who Rakinos said were their enemies.

John had been Rakinos' right hand man and enforcer for years now, and Rakinos always seemed like the only father he had ever had. John had respected him, looked up to him. Rakinos had personally taken an interest in him years ago and had groomed him to be the man he was today, but something was breaking in that relationship now. Now, all Rakinos did was hide things from him, treating him more and more like one of his experiments, one of his tools.

A shadow moved in the darkness to John's left shattering his thought stream and he turned, his yellow eyes glaring in the dark and saw Rakinos step into the room.

"Updates? The four soldiers are ready. Madison is still alive. The prototype could be our field leader since he is the most stable. We have five converts total now that so far have survived." Rakinos told him, a deep hunger in his voice, a dark and twisted energy that John hadn't heard before.

So, he's turned another shifter into one of those things, three wasn't enough, experimenting on Madison wasn't enough, John thought and swallowed his words.

John glanced at the screens and then turned back to Rakinos.

"We've tracked them to Carsonville and back and they just left The Wolves Den and are heading out of the city."

Rakinos frowned. His scarlet eyes burned in the shadows.

"Carsonville...Which direction are they heading out of the city?" Rakinos asked, crossing his massive arms, his face growing dark with thought.

"Northwest."

A smile was born on Rakinos's face, revealing the edges of his pearly white fangs. For the first time, that look genuinely made a shiver run down John's spine.

"I know where they're going. John, I want you to prepare the strike team. It's the perfect time to test our new...recruits. I want Brian MacGregor and Max Mullen taken alive. If anyone else gets in your way, feel free to do what you and your teams do best."

John nodded, at least glad to be moving again as he pushed the thoughts he was having back down into the dark of his mind. He moved past Rakinos and was headed out the door when he paused and turned.

"Where are we headed?" he asked.

Rakinos took a deep breath almost as if he were savoring the thought. He looked away from John and down at the monitors.

"Forest Glen."

CHAPTER 4

"On a cobweb afternoon
In a room full of emptiness
By a freeway I confess
I was lost in the pages
Of a book full of death
Reading how we'll die alone
And if we're good, we'll lay to rest
Anywhere we want to go..."

--- Audioslave, "Like a Stone."

I thought I was finally beginning to understand.

The thought kept running through Brian's mind on repeat.

It had taken him two weeks to finally get comfortable with his new situation; his new self, his father's hidden past, and now, well hell now his solidarity with what he really was had been thrown out the window. There was something wrong with him after all, something that was dangerous, unpredictable and out of control. It was beginning to sink in that he had killed people. After the fight in the warehouse, the notion hadn't bothered him much because he was riding high on adrenaline, on fear and relief that Max was alive.

Now?

Now he had time to sit and really think about it mostly because he was confronted with the fact that it had very nearly happened again to an innocent person, to one of Max's friends.

How many of those men in the warehouse had died?

How many have died at my hands? He thought looking down at his open palms with their rough finger-pads and black fur, the blunt short claws on the ends of his fingers. In his mind, he had a terrible image of his hands wet with sticky crimson blood and the image was so strong that he found himself wiping his hands on his jeans legs before he could stop himself.

How many? His brain asked again as it chewed the notion like a dog with a rawhide bone.

He knew at least three. Maybe more. His memories flashed through his head, stabbing at him again with their images tainted red, jumbled and confused, out of order, seen from someone else's perspective.

A body flying through the air with a cry of pain, slamming into a piece of heavy machinery, the sound of breaking bone.

A man lying in a broken pile of wood and metal with a neck twisted at an unnatural angle.

A man on his knees…a violent kick…the thump of flesh heavily hitting flesh…

Blood spraying in the air like warm rain from a hellish sprinkler.

The truth was staring him in the face at last.

He was a killer.

I am a killer.

He looked over at Max. How did he handle it? Did it bother him?

Of course, Brian had known that Max had taken lives over the course of his career as a vigilante, and he knew that Max had probably killed those men that had attacked Brian himself. That felt different, disconnected and not so personal. It was more personal, he realized when it was your hands that had done the killing and worse, he didn't even know he was doing it. It was like he had been asleep the entire time, floating in his mind while his body did its own thing.

Brian swallowed down the bile he felt rising in his throat as he thought about what nearly happened at the club with Blaine. He could have seriously hurt him or worse and he had little or no memory of actually putting him on the ground until Max's voice called through the shadows and touched him, snapping him back like a rubber band.

Blaine is nearly twice as big as I am; how did I flip him like a sack of potatoes?

As he was lost in thought, the truck bounced over a rut in the road as it made its way towards Forest Glen. Max was driving and they had left the city behind well over an hour ago.

"Fuck..." he whispered to himself more than anything, putting his face in his hands and rubbing his temples.

"Brian?" Max asked, glancing over at him in the passenger seat before shooting his eyes back on the road.

Brian shook his head at him. "Nothing, just talking to myself."

"No, you're angry and scared. I'm not normally one to talk things out but you showed me the value of that. I trust you. Trust me now. Talk to me." Max said quietly, his eyes dipping down the dashboard instrument panel as they made one of the final turns.

Brian looked up at that admission and his hands fell into his lap as he tried to piece together his thoughts. He sighed.

"I thought I was getting the hang of all this. I thought I finally understood it all. And now there's this...something new. Now it's a whole new damn ball game half way into the eighth fucking inning."

Max sighed and for a moment didn't speak. He was collecting his thoughts and Brian shot a look at him, his green eyes flashing in the now twilight blue of the truck cab as the sun went down outside.

It was obvious that Max was struggling to put together the right words. He wasn't kidding, Brian thought. He wasn't used to talking things out but the fact that he was trying meant more than anything he could say. Max glanced over at him.

"I don't know Brian. I want to say all these nice things and make you feel better but...It feels like I'm lying when I think about it. I've never seen anything like what happened at the club and if that's what happened at the warehouse then, well, I don't know what could be going on."

"I killed people, Max. That's what happened. I'm a killer." Brian said bluntly, his voice rising a little in disgust at himself.

Max shook his head and frowned. "No, you were defending yourself. There's a difference in between a murderer and someone who fights to save others or their own life. You aren't a killer, Brian. You're a survivor."

Brian shook his head. Max wasn't getting it. He sighed and looked out at the road in the headlights.

"It's different when you aren't in control, when you don't know what you are doing. I just wanted to get you out of there. I didn't even stop to check on any of them or even process what had happened. It was so fast. From the moment I set foot on the docks, I felt something was different in me. I was too amped up to realize it but it's been here, in me, the whole time, since I…since I turned." Brian lamented, his voice growing quiet as his eyes wandered out through the windshield at the passing fields and woods of darkened trees as the first stars began to peek out. He almost mentioned the dreams with the stalking shadowy beast but thought he was making himself sound like a lunatic already.

"Sometimes, it's worse when you know what you're doing." Max replied quietly, his eyes far away in thought as he responded.

His words hung in the truck cab, their meaning heavy and not lost on Brian. For the entire remaining trip to Forest Glen, neither of them spoke to the other, each one lost in his own thoughts as true night finally fell. Brian never noticed as they approached the gate to Forest Glen, never noticed as they passed through it and finally seemed to come back to the world as Max pulled his truck to a stop in the circular driveway. As the headlights faded and the truck engine went silent, Brian noticed there were more cars than usual.

He recognized Raven's red sedan but he didn't recognize the deep midnight blue coupe with the tinted windows.

"Who's that? Jackson?" he asked warily, wondering if another Rakinos was waiting for them inside.

Max shook his head. "Nope. Jackson and Molly spend so much time here they just park their cars in the garage. That would be Ash."

That information made Brian turn his head to the side like a curious puppy and when he felt himself do it, he frowned and stopped it.

"Why's he here? I thought he and Draco didn't get along." He asked opening the truck door. Max followed suit and with a thunk of car doors, both of them were ascending the steps to the heavy front door of the house, the porch lights and garden accent lights casting tasteful shadows on them and the hedges, the statuary and making the old house gleam.

"I don't know but if he's here that means something big is going down inside, something big enough to make them talk."

"I hope it's not me. I sorta hope Blaine didn't notice what happened at the club and tell Ash. I don't want to lose my chance at a new start. I just got stabilized and now that's been taken out from under me. I feel like a karmic punching bag." Brian grumbled under his breath.

"Are you going to tell Raven about the memory lapses and what happened in the club? You probably should. If you're in danger..." Max asked as he reached for the door handle.

Brian shrugged his shoulders. Max was right and he could hear the concern in Max's gruff voice.

"I guess I don't have much of a choice. Still a little miffed that you guys didn't tell me about the drug but...I don't know Max. This whole thing keeps getting more complicated every time I think I've gotten it."

Max let go of the door handle and turned to Brian, putting his arms around him and pulling him into a warm embrace. He nestled his muzzle into the thick fur of Brian's neck.

"I really am sorry about that. It won't happen again. Listen to me. I don't care how bad it is, how crazy it gets. We're in this together, got it?" he said quietly, his voice comforting in Brian's ears.

Brian returned the hug and it felt good, like a medicine on a sore throat.

"Yeah. I guess I'm not really mad at either one of you. That's not really what's bothering me. What if I'm a danger to you and everyone else...You saw what happened at the club...If I hurt any of you by accident by losing control again...."

Max let go and looked Brian in the eyes. "I've faced scarier things than you, pup. I think." He added with a small smile. "Look who you're talking to."

Brian nodded and he felt a half-hearted smile try to spread but it got stuck.

"Well, standing out here isn't going to get it over with. Let's get on with it then...and thank you, Max. That means a lot to me. Together."

"Together. Come on, pup."

With that, the two of them entered the manor the door closing behind them with a solid click of the locks and tumblers.

Brian felt his ears perk forward and there was Roy coming around the corner. He was dressed in a flannel shirt with his sleeves rolled up and a pair of old beat up jeans.

"Oi, there ya be, laddie. Good to see ya again. Everyone's in the library waiting on ye." He greeted them, his rich accent warming the air around them instantly like miniature sun. He glanced at Max. "Always good to have ya home, Max."

Nodding, Brian and Max both moved to catch up to him, and it still amused Brian to see Roy. It was like a living walking talking stereotype. He felt the corners of his mouth pick up a bit despite his inner turmoil. The short werewolf with the Scottie mustache walked with them as he matched their pace.

"It's good to see you again, Roy." Max said, noticing that Brian was quickly falling into a depressive quiet and the tension was becoming too much to bear.

"Aye, and you too."

"Ash is here, huh?" Max asked as they walked past the initial parlor where Brian had first met Rakinos and Draco and moved down the hall, past the staircase and turning right past the gymnasium. Roy arched a dark eyebrow and turned his brown eyes on Max.

"He is. Tis a bloody rare thing to get his striped arse up here these days. Imagine it, they aren't even fighting. For now. But you know how that goes." Roy told them as they passed through a wide arch and came to a set of double doors.

"Roy, what's going on?" Brian asked, looking the Scottie house manager in the eyes.

Roy shook his head as he stopped short at the doors to the library.

"Aye, lad, I think it's best if we let the doctors do the talking. I'm not one for this kinda thing. Goes over my head and I don't wanne tell ye wrong but know this: ye be in good hands. We're all behind ya, lad. It's what we do. We protect each other so no matter what ye find out in there, we stick together. This family always has."

With that, Roy swung the double doors wide and they stepped into the main library of Forest Glen.

The writer in Brian peeked out from under the rock it had been hiding under for weeks as he got his first real look at the scope of the room. He had not yet been in the library at Forest Glenn and the first thing he noticed was the sheer number of books. The room itself was two stories high and books lined every square inch of that space. The vaulted ceilings were held up by thick deeply stained and aged wooden braces. Each one was dust free and shined to a mirror finish.

The floors similarly shone and were made of the same dark wood that had to date back to the original house. The shelves were built into the walls and each one was labeled and there was a wide catwalk that ran around the upper shelves of the room connected to a curved spiral staircase to the main floor.

Soft amber accent lights lit the shelves from within giving the thousands of old books a warm glow. Hanging lights from the ceiling lit the rest of the room and there were only soft shadows at the edges of the library. Two giant ornate rugs covered a vast majority of the floor and at one end there was a large fireplace and on the other, a long desk with at least two ultra-modern high-tech computers with two chairs. Each computer was dark for the moment. An entire bank of floor to ceiling windows lined the outside wall, giving anyone in the library a fantastic view of the grounds and woods behind the house and there, far down the fields, the lake shimmered in the rising moonlight. Brian's inner bookworm wept tears of joy but he couldn't feel them properly at the moment out of his nearly needling anticipation.

He felt a soft elbow in his ribs and looked over at his side to see Max giving him a gentle smirk.

"What?" Brian whispered, coming back to the real world.

"I was worried your jaw was going to disconnect." Max replied quietly with a grin.

"Oh." Brian replied and made sure to pick up his jaw from the floor with a flash of embarrassed awkwardness. Despite the funeral-like atmosphere, Max chuckled in spite of himself and that made Brian feel a bit better.

In the middle of the room was a long conference table, lined with ten chairs and in these chairs, Brian saw that everyone had gathered and sat and when the truth sunk that they were all waiting for him, his grin faded as everyone's quiet conversation died away.

He felt his stomach lurch a bit and he felt the attention in the room turn fully onto him, like an ant under a magnifying glass.

Draco sat at the head of the table, his arms resting on the oak wood in a relaxed and open manner. His silver fur shone under the warm lights and his pony tail rested over his right shoulder. He wasn't dressed in a suit this time but was dressed instead in a neat white button-down shirt that was tucked into his dark business pants. He looked every bit like the consummate professional that he was. The top two buttons were open on the collar.

Molly sat at his side, as always in a dark pant suit, this time with a mini-skirt that cut off just above her knees. Her dark blazer was open revealing a clean pressed white blouse underneath. Her gold cross winked in the light as she raised her head to look at him from her phone. She nodded at him in welcome as Brian's eyes found Jackson.

Jackson looked exhausted but his eyes were alert behind his round glasses and they looked nearly wild as if he was barely sitting still. His red shirt was rumpled as were his khaki pants. The fur on his head was also slightly ruffled. He was fiddling with a laptop in front of him, going to town on the keyboard, the clicking of the keys quiet but noticeable.

Brian shot his eyes to the other end of the table where Ash Riley sat, not looking at his brother but rather watching Brian himself. Ash had changed out of his work clothes and was now dressed in a casual blue polo and black jeans. He had kept his piercings in and in the soft light of the room, his gray fur and black tiger stripes were strongly contrasted even more than they were before. His thick arms twitched a bit. It was obvious he was having a hard time being here and he was doing all he could to try and maintain a professional presentation. The tension between the brothers was as noticeable as their resemblance.

Roy had found himself a seat near Ash and there, Brian saw at last, was Raven.

He hadn't seen her in days and honestly, she looked rough. She was currently in her human form. Her chestnut brown hair hung around her shoulders loose, as if not much thought had gone into it. Her eyes were tired and her face looked drawn.

She wasn't in her hospital coat but just a red pull over and a pair of simple black pants. Brian had never seen her so tired and he felt the slightest twinge of guilt for yelling at her earlier. She looked like hell but even then, she looked radiant in her own way.

Draco cleared his throat and his warm rich voice broke the silence as he addressed Brian and Max.

"Please, have a seat, both of you. I'm sorry for having so many people here to discuss the situation but since it would impact everyone here, especially you Brian, you can see the need to keep everyone in the loop. My brother is here because he told me you were one of his new employees. He needs to know as well." Draco said calmly, meeting Brian's eyes.

Brian nodded knowing Draco was right but said nothing as he and Max each took a seat next to each other.

Unable to take the awkward tension any longer, Brian broke it.

"Can someone please tell me what's going on? Why did you want to meet me here? What does that drug have to do with me?" he asked, his voice shaking a little as he looked at Raven.

Nodding and his eyes understanding, Draco replied before Raven could respond.

"I think it's time we all understand what's happening here, you most of all Brian. I think we finally have the answers we weren't able to provide you at first and it does tie into the drug. If you can tell us what you learned from your mother, then what we have learned here may start to come together into a coherent picture."

"How did—" Brian started to ask confused then he realized that from the sheepish look on Jackson's face and the stoic professionalism on Molly's that the two of them had probably been tracking both Max and him after they refused to answer Raven's calls. He sighed.

"Never mind."

He glared at Jackson and Molly both. Jackson seemed to shrink a bit from it but Molly stood her ground.

It's no wonder she was a good agent before she left the FBI, Brian thought. She was like steel.

Taking a breath and putting his emotions and squirming fear, annoyance and the cold nibbling fear in his chest aside, Brian did as he was asked, meeting each eye as he talked. Under the table Max put a reassuring hand on his right thigh and gave a small squeeze. It helped as Brian told them.

"You all know my dad died when I was fifteen. All my life I thought he was a human. My mom was human. I thought I was too. It turns out, both of them were pretty involved in shifter activism before I was born and there was a lot of family drama because my dad as it turns out was a shifter. He…gave it up…I think is the best way to say that… to try and give me a normal life…a life away from everything he and my mom went through. When I was born and got old enough and didn't show any signs of being a shifter, he and my mom decided it was for the best to make sure I didn't know about his past or hers, so they kept up the story. They didn't want me to have to face the stigma and bullshit they did, to see the family drama. So, Raven was right; I did have a dormant shifter gene. From my dad."

Across the table, Raven nodded, and Brian could tell a small feeling of relief went through her. Or maybe it was just an academic enjoying the feeling of being right.

Raven looked at him.

"So, the shifter in your family was your father. That makes sense. In families, the shifter gene is a dominant one. Yours must have been mutated to be dormant, which may explain a few other things." she told him quietly and he noticed she had trouble meeting his eyes.

It was obvious the tension between them was still there, and he wasn't the only one feeling it.

"What do you mean?" Brian asked.

Brian could tell she knew something. They all did. The atmosphere in the room was far too tense, too much on edge. It felt like…Fear.

His voice shaking, he asked the question again. "What did you find…?"

Closing her eyes and taking a breath, Raven opened them and looked at Jackson. She nodded and Jackson stole a quick glance at Brian before doing something on his laptop.

With a click, the center of the table slid apart to reveal a hidden compartment out of which rose a small rounded projector. Brian recognized it as one of the new HoloMax projectors. They were cutting edge tech that could project three dimensional interactive holograms. The hospital had a set of them for diagnostics work in radiology and the MRI lab. There had been talk of them being used in augmented reality video gaming, though for now the tech was still too expensive for most consumers.

With a few keystrokes from Jackson, the projector came to life with a flicker of blue-white light, light that resolved into full color and a moment later, a projection of a DNA strand was hovering above the table in extremely intricate detail. To Brian it looked like every single DNA model he had ever seen with chains of red and blue amino acids.

Raven looked up at the projection.

"That is a normal DNA strand. I'm assuming you know enough about DNA from high school biology to remember the basics. DNA is a carrier of genetic information that is encoded into nucleotides, each one of which is a nucleobase: cytosine, guanine, adenine and thymine. These bases are held together by sugars called deoxyribose and phosphate groups."

As Raven spoke, she stood up, and suddenly Brian felt like he was in a college class again. As she identified each nucleobase, it lit up, each one a different color: red, blue, orange and green. She went on.

"In baseline humans and every shifter that has ever been studied, in fact, in every complex life-form on the face of the planet, this group of nucleotides, bases and pairs always occur in a double helix formation that is zipped and unzipped as proteins carry out the genetic instructions on those bases by RNA."

She looked at Jackson and Jackson made a few keystrokes and the hologram shrunk as a new hologram appeared next to it.

Brian frowned as he stared at it. He had never seen anything like it in his life.

It was a DNA strand or something like one. Instead of the spiral staircase of a double helix however, this strand was truly strange with a third protein strand between the two that were normally there, forming a strange sort of triple helix. This odd strand had all four colors from the standard strand yet this one also had a new nucleobase, one that was highlighted in purple that run up and down the length of the third strand but radiated out to all the other bases as well like a tree branch.

"What is that?" he asked, thoroughly confused.

"That," Raven said, choosing her words carefully, "Is a triple helix DNA strand. Triple helix DNA has only been theorized about since 1953 and back then, it was because at the time, Watson and Crick hadn't yet discovered the structure of a DNA strand. The triple helix was proposed that year by the two of them and a few other scientists. Later that same year, they did end up discovering the structure of DNA which as every geneticist and student is taught, is a double helix ladder."

"So, it's a theoretical construct..." Max asked, leaning in. Science wasn't his strong point but this was all about Brian and he had a sinking feeling starting to come into his gut.

"Not anymore. The first triple helix DNA was observed in 1957 in the reproductive process of E. Coli bacteria, but it dissolved soon after and we still aren't sure why it even happened in the first place. Triple helix DNA could be used in modern medicine for gene therapy to regulate the expression of genetics far more efficiently than splicing; it would allow doctors to weave together different DNA strands, to make hybrid species of plants for better agriculture. But all that has been just theory.... until now."

"Where did you get that from then? What DNA is this?" Brian asked, dreading the answer as a part of him already knew it.

"Yours." She told him quietly as she plunged ahead. Not a peep could be heard in the room as the soft glow from the holograms bathed everyone's faces.

"When I first took your samples weeks ago at the apartment, your hormone levels were surging. At the time, I thought it was because you were about to change for the first time but I was wrong. The hormone surge, the mood swings, all of that was a result of your DNA itself changing in ways that I never considered. When I took your blood again at the manor days ago, I tested your hormone levels and they were normal but that protein, the one I told you about, it was nearly ubiquitous in every sample I tested and I couldn't figure out why or what it was or what it did." Raven told him as Jackson clicked his keys again.

The hologram shifted, getting rid of the one normal strand, leaving Brian's triple helix DNA floating above the table. This time, the purple nucleobase was highlighted.

"When Rakinos was here helping us, or supposed to be at any rate, he ran simulations. We didn't know he had run them because he forcibly wiped them from our system and nearly burned out two of our supercomputer cores downstairs. Jackson and Molly were able to recover the data and this is what they found. Jackson, bring up the normal human DNA sample from Molly."

"I had Molly give us a sample of her DNA to prove what the simulations showed and to be honest, I don't know what to say so I'll let the simulation play for you." She finished.

The triple helix DNA moved to the left and in its place sprang up a normal double helix strand. One of the purple nucleobases from the triple helix strand jumped over to the double helix strand. Suddenly, the entire double helix strand began to fall apart, unzipping at the base pairs. It was like watching a ladder be cut in two and then spread flat but instead of dissolving, the now unzipped DNA began to change. The purple nucleobase began to replicate itself along the fallen strands and soon it began to pull them together again, reinforcing them, strengthening the bonds.

Brian watched open mouthed as the formerly human DNA strand began to change and when it was done, a new triple helix DNA strand floated side by side with the original, purple nucleobase and all.

Realization dawned on him and he felt a shiver run through him.

"Molly doesn't have any shifter heritage...does she?" he asked quietly.

"No, I don't." Molly told him. "If I were to be bitten by a shifter, I would die."

Brian simply sat in his chair, dumbfounded.

"That means that...that purple protein...it ...I...can turn normal people into shifters...." he said more to himself than anyone else.

Raven nodded. "Yes. What I thought was a protein is in fact a new type of nucleobase entirely. Instead of ripping apart the DNA like normal, it actually acts like a form of replicant RNA, restructures the base pairs and allows the DNA to survive. It alters it into a form like your own. Essentially if that was ever done in a live person, that person would be turned into a shifter, just like you but that's not all that this new nucleobase does. It's far more than a simple transcription molecule."

She paused for a moment and looked at Jackson and then at Brian.

"Brian, have you been having memory lapses? Especially when you get emotional or angry? Blackouts?"

Brian felt his heartbeat begin to quicken and his pulse speed up. The flashes of the warehouse came back and hit him hard in the gut. He broke out in goose flesh, the fur on his arms standing up.

"When I went after Max, it happened..." he told her.

"What do you mean you went after Max?" Draco asked suddenly, his eyebrows raising as he looked from Max, to Raven and back to Brian.

Raven suddenly looked very uncomfortable. Brian couldn't help it and snorted at her.

"So, you didn't tell just me then? That makes me feel better." He said bluntly.

"Raven what is he talking about?" Draco asked as he turned to her.

Sighing she looked at Draco and then to Max and settled at last for looking at Draco. Brian watched her stiffen as she spoke.

"You all know that the new drug on the street has been killing people. Normal humans. My team at the hospital was barely making any headway. I've put more people in the morgue in the past two weeks that I have in my entire residency. I couldn't stand to bury one more person without knowing why. I asked the police for information and was rebuffed; they said they had no idea. The drug was the same one that the man was on when Brian and Mr. Connors intervened and if it hadn't been for that drug, Brian wouldn't be here. I asked Max to help me track it to the source so we could contact the police and have them end it before my morgue ended up full."

The silence in the room was powerful, heavy and it made the air feel thick to breathe.

"You asked Max to go out into the streets, alone, to track down this drug and didn't tell any of us?"

"Yes."

"Max, given your...past...I'm assuming you did it and didn't plan on telling any of us that you put yourself in extreme danger, more so than usual?" Draco stated, not even bothering to ask because he knew the answer from reading Max's face.

With a sigh, Draco, threw his hands down on the table and for the first time his tone changed from its gentle warm tones and Brian heard the first hints of surprise, fear and maybe a hint of anger. He leaned on his left hand, fingers under his chin as he thought before he spoke. His hand dropped and he pinned Raven with a look.

"Raven that was absolutely foolish of you to ask that of Max and Max, even though I know what you do in your spare time at night, that was even more foolish of you to do it. I'm glad you're safe and thank you, Brian for following him but I cannot believe how irresponsible all of you acted. All three of you. You two could have been killed and you, Raven, your career could have jeopardized. No mystery is worth it."

Brian noticed that Max wouldn't meet Draco's eyes when he was speaking and was looking down at the table, unusually cowed.

"It won't happen again but I do need to know what you both found there. It may provide answers about that drug." Raven said quietly and honestly.

Max spoke up next, trying to keep his gaze away from the disappointed Draco.

"When I first got there, it was just human gang members. The 86ers. The same guys that went after Brian to begin with. I watched them for a bit and then Rakinos showed up."

Draco sat up straight, his eyes wide. "What?

"Rakinos. He showed up at the docks." Max told him.

"What did he want?" Molly asked, looking from Brian to Max.

Max shrugged. "He started talking to them. Something about them stealing something from him called Wolf's Bane. Must be what that drug is called. Then he made them an offer. Come with him or he kills them. Something about giving them power."

"Then what?" Draco put in, an extremely dark look coming over his face as he looked at Raven, who sat looking like a deer in headlights.

"I don't remember because the next thing I knew I got hit from behind. I wasn't paying attention. I let my temper get in the way and all I could see was Rakinos. I never heard one of his lackeys come up behind me until I was being thrown through a goddamn window. Rakinos told them to kill me slow and bring my head to him. Then he left. After that, it's pretty much a blur...but there's something else."

Max swallowed as he looked up at the triple helix DNA strands floating above the table. The images would flicker once every few seconds.

When he spoke again, he looked at Raven.

"There was something else with him. I don't know what it was. It was huge. Eight, nine feet tall at least. Maybe six hundred, seven hundred pounds of pure muscle. It had a shifter's face only bigger. Its teeth and claws were black. It had some kind of device around its wrist and it had that same blue shit you asked me to find pumping inside. It killed a gang member single handedly without even trying. Punched his heart out and then tore him two. I've never seen anything like it. Took assault rifle rounds like they were air-shot. Didn't even flinch."

Raven blanched and swallowed.

"Of course. Now I understand why Rakinos deleted the simulations he ran. Now I know what he was hiding..." She said and looked at Jackson. "Play the final simulation. Now it makes sense."

Jackson keyed up the final sequence and the hologram changed as the test DNA strand vanished. Now, two models appeared, one marked A and the other B. Each model was the basic shape of a shifter in wolf form.

"Okay, for all intents and purposes, model A is Brian and his triple helix DNA with the new nucleobase, the one marked in purple. Model B is a normal baseline shifter with normal shifter DNA." Jackson said as he finished keying up the simulation.

"This one was the one that was most degraded." He warned her.

"Play it." Raven said solemnly.

Everyone in the room watched as the holograms began to move. First, Model A began to turn red and yellow and orange.

"Each color represents a stress hormone in the flight or fight response: Adrenaline, cortisol and norepinephrine. These are the stress hormones that our bodies make in extreme situations in order to protect ourselves by engaging an automatic flight or fight response. In humans and shifters, this gives us the energy burst to run away or to stand our ground. In some cases, it can give short bursts of extreme strength or stamina. That's how little old ladies can lift cars off of their grandchildren in moments of sheer panic." Raven said as the levels in the Brian model reached their peak.

"Brian, in you, this response is different. The extreme levels of stress hormones seem to interact with and activate the nucleobase instructions and when they do, instead of focusing that autonomic response outward, your body for some reason focuses it inward."

Brian watched in horror as the hologram of him began to change, warping, growing, transforming.

His normal six foot four three-hundred and twenty-five-pound form distorted and began to bulk out even more. His arms grew longer, thicker. His claws extended, his teeth grew. In mere moments, the model that represented him was no longer recognizable as even a basic shifter, let alone himself.

Now the model stood hovering over them all was an eight-foot-high six-hundred-pound plus living tank with a thick broad body that towered over any other person Brian could think of, even Rakinos. The model now had wicked curving claws and gnashing teeth. It was like a hulk, a living breathing super werewolf on steroids, its muscles dense and well defined, its fur the color of space with no markings of any kind. Living darkness turned into a predator.

"Oh my god...." he gasped.

The memory lapses and flashes.

The warehouse.

The club.

"Bleeding Christ above...saints preserve us..." Roy said under his breath, his brown eyes going wide.

"As you can see, once the stress levels hit their peak, they trigger a transformation above and beyond a normal change for a shifter into a secondary form that for all intents and purposes is a living weapon. Extreme strength, speed, stamina, senses, durability beyond reason. The downside to this form is that the sheer levels of stress hormone in the body would prevent most people from behaving rationally." Raven went on. She paused and resumed.

"It would be highly unlikely that in this state, the person could even begin to control themselves. Conscious thought itself may fade away. The adrenaline levels alone would be enough to kill most people. So, I'm asking you again: Brian, have you had any memory lapses or blackouts?"

Brian swallowed looking at the floating hologram in shock. It was the monster from his dreams, the one that stalked him in the shadows. It was the voice that whispered to him, seducing him to let it out.

This time, he didn't avoid the question. When he spoke, his voice was small and shook, barely above a whisper as all eyes in the room fell upon him in that dreadful pregnant silence.

"Yes. In the fight at the warehouse, they caught me by surprise. They held me down and were going to kill Max. He was injured badly...he couldn't fight back. Seeing him there, dying, defenseless, it made me angry...and then I don't remember anything until I was standing over him with bodies all around me..."

"Bodies? I saw a news report about bodies being found in a warehouse. That was you?" Draco asked, understanding dawning on his face.

"Must have been...I don't remember." Brian told him distantly.

"Has it happened any other time?" Raven asked.

Looking at Ash and then to Max, who nodded for Brian to go ahead, Brian told them.

"Yeah. I've seen that thing in my dreams...it stalks me in the shadows there. But when I went to apply with Ash earlier for the job, Blaine, his security chief and I did some sparring, to see if I could cut it. There was a moment when he had me in an arm lock, when I got frustrated. I wasn't doing so well and I felt something slip.... then the next thing I remember was Max calling my name and seeing Blaine on the ground. I nearly pulled his arm out of his socket. Blaine never knew what happened it happened so fast."

Brian looked down the table at Ash who looked thoughtful and was otherwise quiet. Brian could feel himself being studied.

"When Max called my name, for a moment, I didn't recognize him and then I was me again. Something about his voice pulled me back."

Everyone looked at Max as Draco asked him, "Max, do you remember Brian changing forms like the model?"

Max shook his head. "Not exactly. I was out of it by that point in the fight at the warehouse but at the club...Brian..." Max said looking at Brian with a bit of unease on his face.

He went on. "Your eyes...I could tell you were getting angry but your eyes turned white...it's like they lost their irises and pupils and just turned into white eyes like a damn comic book only brighter. That's when I knew something was wrong, especially after you flipped Blaine over your back like he was nothing and he's easily twice your size."

Brian hung his head.

This was too much. It was happening all over again. Just when he thought he had things under control, life threw him a goddamn curveball. He knew the simulation was right. It had to be. That explained the memory lapses, the disconnected feeling he had.

The monster from his dreams was real and worse, he thought, despair and disgust and terror shooting through him all at once, worse, the monster was him. It was inside him and he could become it at any moment if he lost control. Every person in the room was in danger.

"Brian are you okay?" Draco asked gently as he could, reaching a hand over and placing it on Brian's shoulder. For a moment, Brian didn't answer, his fear threatening to overcome him.

He shook his head no.

"Not really..." he said. Taking a deep breath, he forced himself to sit up. "What happens to model B?"

Raven nodded and continued.

"This new form is transmissible. If that nucleobase that's in your DNA is applied to a shifter that already has an active shifting gene, they will become like you, able to become a living weapon." Jackson added as he pressed a few buttons and the purple protein moved over to Model B and moments later, Model B transformed further as well.

"What about shifters with a mutated gene, like Max?" Brian asked, panic rising in his throat. Max suddenly seemed to remember that Brian had bitten him to help him heal and swallowed.

"After I got back from the fight, I was in pretty bad shape. Brian bit me to induce healing. I didn't know that was a thing but it worked." Max told them, looking at Raven for answers.

"That actually worked? I have no idea why it did ...but I'd wager that based on the simulations Rakinos ran, you'll be fine. A shifter with a mutated shifting gene like yours Max wouldn't be affected to the best of my knowledge though it's hard to say if there would be any effects. Perhaps the rapid healing was a side effect. I'd need to run tests to find out more. Have you had any memory lapses?" She asked him.

Max shook his head. "No. I haven't."

She nodded. "Good. Let's count that as a blessing so far."

"So..." Brian said, sitting back in his chair, dumbfounded. "What does my situation, Rakinos and that drug have to do with each other? Why would he hide the simulations? I don't get it."

"What's that red furred bastard up to?" Max snarled at the name.

Draco sat the far end of the table, his face dark and crossed with worry and something else that may have been regret.

"Luckily for you both," she said looking at Max and Brian, "I do have a hypothesis on that." Raven said. "And there may be way to help Brian deal with his... problem...but first. Rakinos. There is some bad news."

Brian groaned. "What now?"

Molly pitched in, leaning forward.

"Rakinos did more than just hide the simulations. He also stole both of your samples when he left. Raven found them missing not long after you all left. Our guess? He knows about the triple helix and the mutative factor that your DNA has in it. We think he wants to create more of these super-beings but most likely they'd be hard to control. Raven's testing indicated the drug, the "Wolf's Bane" has hypnotic and addictive properties and its custom made for shifter biology it seems. It's the only logical next step; The drug would work as a control agent, making the perfect living weapons."

Brian swallowed as the implications sunk in.

Draco sighed.

"All we have is speculation; we don't know WHY he wants to do this but that leaves us with two major problems to deal with going on those assumptions. The first is obvious: Brian. Now that we know what triggers this state, we need to find a way for him to keep it suppressed until we can understand it better, and I think he will agree it's for his best interests as well as ours. Is that a fair thing to assume, Brian?"

Brian nodded. "Yeah. I suppose it is. I don't want to hurt anyone, especially any of you. I'll do whatever's needed."

"What's the second problem?" Max asked, having a suspicion as to where this was going and he didn't like it.

"Rakinos is the second problem. I have a terrible feeling, whatever his agenda, that he isn't done with us yet. Brian, you are in extreme danger. We need to take precautions. I fear the police may be out of their element in this regard, especially given the nature of shifter relations at present." Draco finished and sat back heavily in his chair.

Max growled deep in his throat. It was a low and penetrating sound, a sound of anger and rage.

Jackson piped up a thoughtful look on his face as he looked at Raven. "About Brian's problem, I was thinking. Do you know that new medical bracelet that they put out for diabetics that tracks their insulin level and then doses them as needed?"

Everyone turned to him and Raven nodded. "Yes?"

"Well, what if I could modify or build one to track Brian's adrenaline levels, once it hits a threshold, it will automatically dose him with a safe amount of sedative, just enough to get him calm again but not to knock him out?" he postulated.

Brian thought about that. "That actually sounds like a good idea. Could you do it? Would it work?"

Jackson shrugged. "If Raven would help me with the medical parts, the hardware and software should be easy enough."

Raven agreed. "It should. We can't do much about Rakinos yet but this is something we can try to make headway on. We have the parts here and a 3D printer."

Draco nodded. "Good, make it a priority. As for now, I think we all need a break. It's been a revealing meeting and I think we could use some time to process all of this, especially Brian. I know I have much to consider about these developments. "

"Agreed. My ass is getting sore sitting here listening to all the medical talk." Ash said, standing up, rubbing feeling back into his legs. He didn't look at Draco but he paused at Brian and looked at him.

"Don't worry about your job, man. I'm not getting rid of you for this mess. I think these nerds," he said with the slightest bit of gentle sarcasm, "I think they'll figure it out and get you sorted. I still want you at work next Friday, hulk wolf or no hulk wolf. Don't worry about Rakinos either." His voice darkened as he glanced at Draco. "We'll find a way. My brother here is good at getting out of messes."

Draco's ears flattened but he did not reply.

"Is that what we're calling it? Hulk Wolf?" Jackson asked, his ears perking up excitedly.

"No." Brian and Raven both told him simultaneously. Jackson looked a little disappointed.

Ash clapped him on the shoulder and left the library, heading towards the kitchen with a sigh, leaving Brian sitting there feeling very small but at least not totally dejected, but the fear that a terrorist and a gang were both hunting him now was eating at him.

When was life going to slow down and just be life again?

"I'm going to go run a systems check on the security system. I want to be prepared for anything at this point." Molly said and got up and headed out of the library and headed left up the hallway.

"I'm going to head to tech room and see if I can work up the schematics on that bracelet. Brian, I may need you to come by in a few for a measurements. I can probably print the thing out if we can get the medical parts down. Raven?" Jackson asked as he closed his laptop and powered down the projector.

Raven looked at him, nodding.

"Sure. I'll be there in a few minutes. I need to talk to Brian alone for a few if that's okay."

Roy and Jackson both got up and were out the door together. As he walked past, Roy gave Brian's shoulder a friendly squeeze and a nod. With everyone gone, Draco, Max, Brian and Raven sat alone at the table. Draco motioned at Max.

"Max, I need a word in private. Can I see you outside?"

Max's ears dropped but he nodded and followed Draco out of the room with a glance back at Brian who nodded at him that he would be fine.

At last, Brian and Raven were alone together and for a time, they sat apart from each other, neither speaking.

Raven finally broke the awkward silence.

"Brian...I don't know what else to say but that I'm sorry I didn't trust you. You trusted me from the start and I should have shown you the same courtesy. It was wrong of me. It was stupid."

Brian, surprised at her blunt honesty, took a breath and nodded. "Yeah it was. Raven, I'm not afraid of danger. I'm not afraid to get hurt. It mostly made me angry because my dad would hide things from my mom and me, things from his work and it put distance between us but I shouldn't have taken out my past on you either. Max... Max is special to me. I was just afraid..." He said the last part slowly and carefully.

Raven's eyes widened. A tiny smile crossed her face despite the dour mood.

"I thought something was different between the two of you. I could sense it. You love him don't you?"

Brian tried to dodge the question, his face starting to burn.

"That is not the point, Raven—"

"But you do...and he loves you too." She pressed.

Brian told her, his face flushing hotter than ever.

"Yeah..." he admitted and when she didn't laugh, he found the courage to go on. "We've really connected in the past two weeks. Something changed and... he's amazing. I can't explain it any more than that."

Her awkwardness from earlier faded away and Raven was smiling again, the same smile Brian was used to.

"Are you guys officially...you know...together?"

Brian glared at her but finally relented. "Yeah...I think we are."

She laughed, gently and warmly, the darkness of the meeting lifting temporarily.

"I knew it. I absolutely knew it. He's been acting strange for a while now, and every time it was around you. I didn't mean to get off track but...that's really awesome. I'm glad for it. He's been alone for a very long time and seeing him like he has been recently, minus the past few days where you guys were MIA, he's been better. Stronger, more confident. I can see it in his walk. You seem to really be what he needed. I've known him for years but this is the first time I've ever seen him walk without looking like the world is around his neck like a chain."

Brian stood up and rested his arms on the back of the chair and smiled. Her words and thinking about Max pushed the worry down a bit. Roy and Max's words came back to him.

Together. Family. Support.

Whatever came, he wouldn't be alone. It helped to know that. A lot.

"So...." He said quietly. "About that fight.... I'm sorry, Raven."

Raven got up and came over to him and Brian turned to her.

"Me too. It won't happen again. It was stupid of me." She told him.

"Awesome. You want to go down and help Jackson with that bracelet? I don't want to wolf out like that anymore." Brian suggested, trying to force a smile onto his face. He wanted to smile for real but he was finding it harder to do than he expected with conflicted feelings running around in his head and heart in marathons.

"Sure." Raven said and he followed her out of the library and as they made their way towards to the tech lab, Brian looked over and saw Draco and Max deep in conversation though he couldn't make out what they were saying. Max saw Brian looking and nodded at him, his blue eyes reassuring him.

Sighing, Brian turned his attention back to following Raven. One thing kept looping through his mind as they walked.

Change is the only constant.

CHAPTER 5

""...Now was acknowledged the presence of the Red Death. He had come like a thief in the night...and darkness and decay...the Red Death held illimitable dominion over all."

- Edgar Allen Poe, "The Masque of the Red Death." (1842).

"What were you thinking?"

Draco asked Max quietly but forcefully as they stood off to the side of the library, leaving Raven and Brian inside alone. Draco stood before Max, his arms crossed and Max was before him, not meeting his eyes, his ears pasted to his head, his face burning but a part of him still argued.

"I do it every night. It's not like its anything new for me." Max replied, a slight rise of emotion as his voice became defensive.

Draco shook his head. "I know you do and I wish you wouldn't. I've asked you to stop before. I know what it means for you, out there-"

Max suddenly looked up at Draco and their eyes did meet.

"No, Draco, you don't. If I'm not out there, people, including shifters like us, they suffer. The gangs prey on them, the law looks the other way because they aren't rich like-" Max felt himself begin to say something he would regret and quickly canned it.

"Like me." Draco finished for him, his ears laying back a bit. Max huffed through his nose and turned away from Draco, looking instead at the painting on the wall. Max didn't recognize it and it didn't matter. What mattered is that right now looking into Draco's ocean-blue eyes was too hard. Getting kicked in the face was preferable. Max could hear something in Draco's voice that cut deeper than any bullet or knife ever could.

Disappointment and sadness.

That notion was the deadliest bullet of all and it always found its mark, Max thought, a deep frown cutting across his features as his ears felt like they were on fire.

Brian and Raven's voices were muffled through the walls as the silence between father and surrogate-son grew strained until at last Draco broke it.

"Max... please...look at me."

Sighing, Max turned to face his mentor.

"I know that you do what you do because you don't want to feel the pain of your past. It's your way of dealing with the ghosts. I know it's dangerous and I know I can't stop you. I just want you to be safe and come home when you're through. One day, I want it so that you don't have to fight those ghosts anymore, but until then, please, do one thing for me? Be more careful."

"I disappointed you, I know. I should have said something." Max said, not looking Draco in his eyes but rather looking at his shoulder.

Draco pulled his head back and cocked it unconsciously a bit. A moment later, his ears fell to the side as he smiled warmly.

He reached out and put a hand on Max's shoulder.

"No, Max. I'm not disappointed in you. What I am, is scared for you. You, Raven, Jackson, even Molly and Ash, you all are the only family I have left. I've lost so much and I know you have, too. I can't stand to lose anymore. I can't lose the only son I've ever had."

His words made Max look up and their eyes met. Draco gave him a strange smile.

"Especially not when he's finally found a spark of happiness in his life that he's so desperately needed." Draco finished and squeezed Max's shoulder.

Max felt his spine stiffen and a mental splash of cold water hit him. The library doors opened as Raven and Brian came out, both of them heading for the tech lab. Brian turned and met Max's gaze. Max felt his heart jump and in spite of himself, he felt the urge to grin but swallowed it, giving Brian a silent nod instead as he and Raven rounded the corner, leaving Draco and Max alone again.

"See what I mean?" Draco asked gently, watching them leave and then looking back at Max.

Max frowned and opened his mouth to protest but then when he saw Draco's smile, he stopped.

"It's that obvious?" he asked meekly.

"You could say that. You've been different ever since he showed up. You've been smiling, and when he looks at you or you look at him, your entire posture and presence changes, Max. I don't think I've ever seen you this engaged and happy and if I may say so, it makes an old man very proud, son." Draco told him and at that last word, Max felt the heat of embarrassment and fear of disappointment leave his body. It was replaced instead by a warm gentle understanding, not only of the time between Draco and himself but rather where he really stood with Draco and he finally understood why Draco had pulled him aside.

"So... I didn't disappoint you too badly then, huh?" Max asked, uncharacteristically uneasy of himself.

Draco raised an eyebrow. "No, just scared me. I know that eventually you'll be back out there and maybe you're right in some ways. Just remember, you don't have to go at it alone. Not anymore. Now....things are different. You have something more to live for if you take it."

Max followed Draco's line of sight and both of their gazes fell upon where Brian had been a moment before.

Max felt a smile tug at the corner of his mouth.

"Yeah...things are different, aren't they?"

Draco nodded silently.

"If I can give you one piece of advice, father to son so to speak," Draco began, waiting for Max.

"Sure." Max replied as Draco turned and headed for the kitchen. Draco had a brother that needed talking to or trying to at least.

"You are never alone and all of us, we're all right here. I'm right here. Don't ever let it go." Draco said and turned, and a moment later he was around the corner, leaving Max to think in the silence of the warm wood paneled hallway.

Max turned a bit and looked at the painting a bit closer. It was a piece he had never seen anywhere else and as many times as he had been at the manor he had never really paid any attention to it. Fine art wasn't his thing.

It was an oil painting of an ocean landscape surrounded by trees and white beaches with a sunrise on the orange horizon. In it, two figures in shadow were frozen in a single moment in time and when he saw the name, he smiled.

Reunited with the Father.

Forest Glen, Rakinos thought.

Even as he looked at it from the cover of the tree line, he felt his upper lip curl, exposing a fang. It was a giant old manor house, designed and built by Draco's father who himself had been an architect and a Scottish immigrant. He had designed the house and grounds as a peaceful haven for his family in a rapidly changing world. He had also designed many of the older buildings in Dawson City and even quite a few in places as far away as New York City. The grounds were well kept, clean and manicured, kept pristine by Roy Campbell, Draco's long-time family friend and estate caretaker, according to the intel.

The lake sat under the light of the moon, shimmering like a gateway to another world.

Draco sat here in his castle and tried to make the world a better place for shifters and humans. *What did he know about how the real-world works?* Rakinos thought distantly. He who was born with a silver spoon in his mouth. He had never known hardship.

Well, except his sister. Death can teach lifelong lessons.

Rakinos smiled a bit to himself. That was only a primer compared to the full lesson in harsh reality that he was about to teach the old man. Of course, the primary goal was the capture of Brian MacGregor and Max Mullen; both were needed for his goals. Anyone else was a walking causality, breathing on borrowed time.

He turned his head, his red eyes gleaming in the darkness as he took in his forces. There were at least twenty shifter soldiers, each fully dressed in jet black combat armor and each one carrying a carbon black HK G36 rifle. He admired them; it had taken him years to build up his weapons trade to the point that he could get them and now, he drank in their lethality. Each one was capable of firing over 750 rounds a minute and with the expanded capacity magazines, laser holographic sights and recoil reducing compensators, each shifter soldier was a walking living weapon.

Twenty pairs of gleaming yellow eyes stared back at him in the dark and there behind them, Rakinos thought, feeling a surge of pride, were the real living weapons.

His Dog Soldiers.

Four hulking monstrosities loomed in the shadows behind the troops. Each one was over eight feet high and thickly muscled, their heavy deadly arms ending in curving seven-inch wicked black claws. He could see them snarling in his blue-grey night vision and knew their black fangs were ready for blood. He could hear them breathe.

They sounded like angry horses; it was a deep rumbling sound.

He had outfitted them in specially designed armored survival combat pants, another perk of having Madison's credentials, even if the good doctor himself was quite incapacitated. Rakinos glanced down to the right wrist of the creatures and was pleased to see the auto-injector monitors that had been grafted there were functioning perfectly.

Each auto-injector functioned as a monitor, keeping track of the stress hormone levels as well as keeping track of the levels of Wolf's Bane currently in their systems. The clear chamber with blue fluid on their wrists glowed in the dark. Each monitor was grafted directly into the circulatory system of the Dog Soldier who wore it, providing it with a steady stream of performance enhancing hypnotic drugs, keeping them in control but deadly at the same time.

What little humanity they had left, if any, was completely subsumed by the rage that their now gigantic malformed bodies were dying to unleash, hatred and anger fueled by chemistry.

He looked at the one that had been the younger shifter, Alex.

It saw him and snarled, growling low in its throat, its mismatched gold and blue eyes gleaming in the dark. It may have growled but it was loyal. It simply had no choice.

Good, Rakinos thought.

He turned to face John who blended into the shadows like living darkness.

"John, situation report." He demanded quietly.

John came up to Rakinos, standing at his side, his arms crossed, casting an eye at the warmly glowing mansion in the distance. He too was in combat armor, his twin yellow eyes gleaming like miniature suns.

"All four dog soldiers show levels within your specified parameters. They'll fight for you. Die for you if they have to. Injectors seem stable. The men are ready and know what they have to do. Capture and extract the two targets and anyone else is expendable. Demolitions packages are ready."

Rakinos looked over John's shoulder at the hulking beasts and a small smile crossed his blood red face. "They seem to follow you, the Dog Soldiers. That's the mark of a leader. Just like we programmed them."

A quick flash of disgust shot across John's face but he squashed it fast; even still, Rakinos noticed it.

John did not care for the Dog Soldier concept. Rakinos had flash trained them with John as their "pack leader" despite John's protest. Something about them had bothered his old right hand and what it was, Rakinos didn't know nor did he care. As long as John did as he was ordered, there would be no complications and John could have whatever fucking opinion he wanted to. John had been responsible on getting the publicly available blueprints for Forest Glen, as well as securing the satellite imagery.

He had a knack for intelligence gathering and each soldier knew the house inside and out now. John had done his briefings well regardless of how he felt. Besides, John and the others, would not disappoint. Rakinos had his own ways to ensure that.

Rakinos turned his attention back to John.

"What's the status of the security system and where are our soon to be hosts?" Rakinos asked, turning back towards the manor. John raised a thermal camera to his eyes and adjusted the viewfinder. A few beeps later, he lowered it and looked at Rakinos, his yellow eyes glinting in the orange glow of the viewfinder.

"Separated; Target one is in the tech room. Target two is in the front entrance way. Everyone else is spread out."

"Security system?" Rakinos replied sharply. Behind him, one of the soldiers who happened to be a technical wizard held up a palm sized tablet and with a few keystrokes, looked up and met Rakinos and his red eyes.

"Neutralized." The smaller shifter replied confidently.

Rakinos nodded. "Well then, I think it's time we go up and say hello."

With a wave of his hand, the military force moved out of the tree line and began to cross the open field towards the house at a full sprint, the dog soldiers loping behind them like giants out of a bygone age risen again from the forgotten mists of time and nightmares.

#####

Draco entered the kitchen quietly and found his younger brother leaning on the counter island, sipping on a beer. The black tile and white counters and stainless-steel appliances gleamed. Ash's grey fur with his black tiger stripes stood out strongly in the clean room as his piercings glinted in the overhead lights.

"Hello, Ash." Draco tried gently as he approached the island and stood on the other side, trying to be as unimposing as possible.

Ash sipped his beer and raised his head to look at Draco. He scoffed a bit.

"So, big brother hunts me down to try and have the talk again. Well," Ash said, taking a long draw off of his beer, "Let's hear it then. What new pitch have you got this time?"

Draco winced. Ash was a little buzzed already. His tolerance was always lower than most. Draco wondered how many he could have downed. Probably way too many, way too fast.

"We don't have to do this, Ash."

"Don't we? I made it clear I didn't want involved in your politics and WHAM!" Ash slammed his hand down hard on the counter top, the sound loud in the room. "Here we are. What a coincidence."

Draco frowned as he sighed. "I didn't intend for you to get involved this time, Ash. None of us intended for this to happen. "

Ash snorted. "Sure. It's not your fault. You never intended for our sister to die either. Sometimes the best fucking intentions have the worst consequences, big brother. You ever heard that? Wise words." Ash snapped back, draining his beer and throwing the glass bottle into the trashcan where it exploded into a thousand pieces when it smashed into the two already in there.

Draco felt the spike stab into his heart from those words and that ghostly gunshot seemed to echo again.

"What happened to Barbara isn't Brian's fault. Don't blame him for it."

Ash crossed his arms and leaned up against the wall.

"Oh, I'm not blaming him for it. You dragged him into this bullshit, just like you did her by getting tangled up with that psycho asshole. Why do you have to share your misery with everyone else, Drake? Why can't you just keep it to yourself, like the rest of us do?"

"That's not fair, Ash. I was trying to help, that's all. I try to help people as best as I can, the same as you do." Draco said, rounding the counter isle where he stopped and looked at his younger brother with something between a mix of longing and pain with the first hints of anger.

"I get people on their feet and send them on their way. You help them and somehow convince them of your great crusade. You don't even have to try. I don't know how you do it." Ash huffed, running a hand through the fur on his head.

Draco opened a cabinet and pulled out a tumbler. He set it down on the counter island and reached into the fridge and pulled out an amber bottle and filled the tumbler half way and put the bottle back. He picked up the glass and drained half of it. He was starting to feel his own temper rise. They had done this dance a hundred time and right now, his nerves were on edge enough. He didn't need this. When he spoke next, his words were strained.

"I'm trying to make a difference so that one day we can all live in a world where Barbara isn't taken from us. There are a thousand Barbara's every day, Ash. If we stand by and do nothing to change it, then there will be thousands more. I can't stand by and do nothing."

Ash stepped forward and got up into Draco's face, speaking through gritted teeth.

Draco could smell the alcohol on his breath.

"She trusted you. I trusted you. Look where we are now. Look where she is now. Six-foot underground because surprise, Drake, the world doesn't give a shit. Our family paid the price because of you."

For a moment, Draco hung his head as his hand holding the tumbler began to shake. Ash noticed it.

"Are you mad? You should be. Let yourself feel it once in a while, for fuck's sake. You never grieved for her. You just dug deeper into your movement and forgot all about her!" Ash pushed and finally Draco snapped.

With a roar of rage, he threw the tumbler across the room where it smashed into a wall, exploding violently into glass shards. He rounded on Ash, his normally gentle eyes moist and angry. His voice shook with his emotions.

"What do you want me to do, Ash? I can't bring her back. I want to, every day. I see her face in my dreams at night. I see her every time one of you step out that door. I see her face every time you open your bar because I don't know what's going to happen to any of you. I see it when Max is on the streets. I don't want to lose any of you, do you understand that? You all are all I have left but I can't sit back and do nothing!"

Ash stood there his face locked in an angry frown to match his brother's and in that moment, brother stood against brother until finally, Draco's shoulders slumped and he leaned against the counter and looked at the wood grain, not meeting Ash's gaze, knowing that on some level, Ash was right and it bothered him.

"Look....Ash. I can't do this anymore. We're all we have left of our family here. I don't want to lose you, too but I can't just not help people who need it. Barb wouldn't have wanted us at each other's throats."

For a moment, Ash stood over him, arms crossed, eyes glinting, chest heaving in anger until finally with a heavy sigh, he turned away from Draco and let his arms fall to his sides. His next words were a quiet admission.

"I know."

Draco looked over at him.

"When our father built this place, then when we built the shelter under the club together, we built them as symbols of hope, beacons in the dark for those who have nowhere else to go. We both agree on that. It helped you get turned around. It helped me mourn in my own way. I need you to understand that I never meant to drag you back into this or to put Brian in the crosshairs. I had no idea that Rakinos was involved in the way he seems to be. I should have never trusted him." Draco said quietly.

Turning around to face his older brother, Ash for a moment, locked eyes with him.

"I'm not blaming Brian for any of this and I guess, I'm not blaming you either but I just want you to know that I can't handle any of this political shit because I've seen it tear apart our family. You and Roy are the last ones left. Mom and dad left years ago. They couldn't handle it either."

Nodding, Draco sighed. "Will you help me help Brian? He needs stability. He needs that job. He needs the exposure to our culture, he needs a foundation. That's all I'm asking you and then I'll never involve you again."

With a sigh, Ash replied quietly, looking at his feet. "I guess but no more, Draco. Please."

Draco nodded in silence as Ash turned to leave the kitchen.

Draco could only look at the shattered tumbler on the ground and wonder if the cup would ever come back together again.

#####

Brian sat in a black plastic chair in the tech room and looking around, he had to admit, even he was impressed. He had never been in this part of the mansion before and it was certainly different from the rest of the house with its floor to ceiling transparent walls which Jackson told him proudly were made of bullet proof glass. The black steel and hyper modern computers and monitors that lined the walls and the desks were something straight out of science fiction movie. A raised glass and metal platform in the center of the room contained twin curving desks upon which sat even more terminals and it was here that Jackson was, standing, working his keyboards, touching screens and moving windows as Raven worked on the medical part of this crazy idea they had.

"So, I'm thinking I'm going to call it an inhibitor bracelet," Jackson said proudly as he picked up some kind of rounded tool with a handle and came back over to Brian. Raven moved aside for him as he continued talking.

"This is a laser scanner. I'm going to use it to get your measurements and then in turn, once we get the programming right, we can use those measurements to begin the 3D printing part and finish fabrication." He nodded over to the corner of the room where a large 3D print system was set up. "I like to tinker with this kind of stuff anyway."

Jackson shoved the open end of the circular loop around Brian's right wrist and with a click of a switch on its side, thin blue beams of cold light appeared and buzzed around Brian's wrist.

"What about when I shift, won't the measurements change?" Brian asked, watching Jackson work.

Raven stopped what she was doing and turned around to face the two of them.

"I thought you couldn't shift?"

Brian met her eyes and gave her a shit eating grin as he transformed right then and there, his wolf form flowing away like black water, receding into himself and a moment later, he sat there in his human form, his brown hair a bit messy and his eyes slowly fading back to amber brown. His clothes hung off of him a bit he noticed; Max had let him borrow some things again and had even let him borrow a pair of his Under-Armor underwear, the kind with the tail loop in them and Brian had to admit, they felt amazing, the sheer fabric snugly hugging his body while not tugging or pulling his fur. It felt even better now on his bare skin.

Raven's eyebrows shot up in shock.

"Since when have you been able to do that?" she asked incredulously as Jackson stood gaping. Brian realized that Jackson had never actually seen him in human form before.

"Hey." He said to Jackson good naturedly.

Jackson stood slack jawed, his face red for some reason as Brian transformed back into his wolf form and a second later, the muscle bound black-furred green-eyed wolf was back.

Jackson collected himself. "You're messing up my measurements! Sit still! We can add in an adjustable locking mechanism though that may make the water proofing more difficult..." he said as he restarted his measurements again.

"Sorry." Brian chuckled.

"Show off," Jackson shot back at him with a tiny grin.

Raven appeared at his side again, needle in hand as she prepared to get a blood sample. "Again, how long have you been able to do that?" She asked, taking up a position next to him. She positioned her needle just below the blood pressure cuff on his upper arm.

"Since I was at my mom's; I finally got the hang of it there. I think it was psychosomatic, not anything physical that was stopping me. It's easy now. I don't know how...I just...you know...*do*."

Raven scowled at him. "That information is important, MacGregor. I need to know these things. As your physician-"

Brian looked up at her mischievously. "Since when?"

"Since now." She said and a moment later, he felt the sharp prick of a needle.

"Watch it!" he yelped in surprise.

"I am watching it, thank you. Perfect bullseye. This should be the last sample I need for a while so we can get a baseline for you and your..." she seemed to get lost, looking for the name of whatever Jackson had called it.

"Inhibitor bracelet!" Jackson called from his work station where he had gone back to, not looking up from his screen.

"That thing." Raven finished. She waited for the tiny hole to close up in Brian's arm and activated his blood pressure cuff. "Try to sit still. We need a solid baseline if this is going to work."

Brian rubbed his arm as the cuff began to tighten with a whir. As the cuff tightened a thought occurred to him and his face darkened.

"You know I don't want to be that thing...it scares the hell out of me. Why are both of you so eager to lock it out though?" Brian asked as the cuff got tighter, squeezing his bicep like a python, making him wince a bit.

Raven sighed and turned around to him.

"Because based on the simulations not only would you probably not have any rational control or even know what you are doing, there's a small chance that once the reaction got going, that it couldn't be reversed. It's a small chance...but it's there." She told him all playfulness suddenly gone.

Brian gulped, a lead weight settling into his stomach.

"You mean...I could get stuck as that thing?"

Raven nodded. "Potentially. Until we know more under safe conditions, I'd like to keep it from showing up again."

Brian swallowed as the cuff relaxed and beeped. "Me too." He said quietly.

"HEY!"

Jackson's surprised yelp caused both Raven and Brian to swivel their heads towards him.

"What?" Raven asked, looking around for something to be on fire or something about to explode.

"What's up?" Brian asked, standing, taking the cuff off of his arm, frowning at the younger shifter who was standing over his keyboards with a surprised and frustrated look on his face.

Jackson stood back and threw up his hands.

"I don't know. Something just glitched in the system and I lost all my work. That shouldn't be possible."

Both Raven and Brian walked up onto the platform and stood next to him looking down at the computer screens and to Brian's surprise, he saw that Jackson was right. Instead of the futuristic looking custom OS that Jackson had been working with when Brian first came in, all that was showing now was a classic blue screen of death.

"Uh, Jackson...what's happening?" Brian asked as he looked around the room. Every monitor, every computer system was flashing to a blue screen of death, each system crashing with multiple fatal errors. The whole system seemed to be crashing and coming down.

"What the hell..." Jackson said in shock, looking around as every terminal in the room went dead with a hiss of electrical sparks and a second later with the unique finality of a generator being disconnected, the lights went dark and the entire room was thrown into pitch black silence.

Their glowing eyes were the only lights left in the room, two yellow, two purple and two green.

"Let's see if we can find Draco. Maybe a fuse blew or something..." Jackson said and led the way out of the tech room with Brian and Raven bringing up the rear, the moonlight coming through the windows aiding their blue-grey night vision. The sliding door that led into the tech room had slid open automatically as a safety precaution the moment the power died and so they had no issues getting out of the room itself.

Brian felt his stomach crawl and the fur on the back of his neck stand up. Something wasn't right. They went down the dark hallways and soon came to the foyer with its large windows and thick front door.

There, Max stood in the foyer, as confused as they were.

"What the hell did you do this time, Jackson?" Max asked, his yellow eyes gleaming in the dark.

"It wasn't me! I swear it! Something knocked out the tech lab and then the whole damn house." Jackson said frowning at the bigger werewolf.

Footsteps caught their attention.

"It wasn't him. Someone cut the power at the main line. Phones are dead too." Molly said, her voice coming from up at the top of the stairs, the silver moonlight from outside turning the inside of the once warm and inviting foyer silver. She carefully made her way down the stairs, a small pen light on her hands.

Swiveling the light from each face in the room, she heard Draco and Ash come up behind them from the kitchen area.

"What happened?" Draco asked as Ash appeared at his side, his wild tiger stripes breaking up his appearance in the deep shadows.

Looking out the window, Ash shook his head.

"Looks like the power is out across the grounds. All the garden lights are off. The pool too." He said.

Brian looked around and suddenly that bad feeling just got worse as the security guard in him knew that something was wrong. As everyone stood in the large foyer trying to figure out what happened, a tiny motion caught his eyes. At first he was confused as he saw it because it made no sense.

It was a tiny red dot, maybe the size of a gnat or a fly and it was hovering over Ash's head.

Then he realized what it was.

"GET DOWN!" he screamed and threw himself at Ash, catching him totally by surprise. Brian's heavier frame knocked the other werewolf to the ground as gunfire exploded, bullets ripping into the window as glass flew like millions of tiny deadly missiles.

Brian felt the heat of each round as it flew over him, barely missing his spine, lifting the fur there as each searing hot lead projectile screamed past him slamming into the stairway, chewing deeply into the wood turning it into Swiss cheese.

By the time Brian and Ash dragged themselves out of the line of fire, shock on their faces, the world had gone insane.

Bullets filled the air, smashing into the walls, paintings, exploding vases and glass cases sending everyone sprawling and scattering them to find cover.

As Brian raised his head, the gunfire stopped and outside he heard heavy booted footfalls coming up the gravel road. He saw dark shadows there with gleaming yellow eyes and he tensed himself for the front door to come crashing down.

Instead, the wall to their right exploded violently in fireball with debris filling the air, the shock wave throwing him and Ash across the room. All sound stopped. For the moment, he was deafened by the extreme sound, the roar of the blast and its shockwave. He saw Molly take cover by spinning herself into a crouch behind the heavy wood half-wall of the upper landing. He saw Max shove Raven and Jackson out of the way and he thought he saw a silver flash, maybe Draco, he couldn't tell because at that moment he was slammed into a wall with a bone splintering crunch and saw stars as he crashed to the floor. Thousands of pieces of sharp shrapnel and debris pelted him, pieces and bits of hot sheetrock and brick. He covered his face as it rained down and when it finally stopped he cracked his eyes open and felt his heart jump into his throat.

Black armored soldiers armed with assault rifles flooded into the gaping hole that had been the library as pieces of books and burning embers rained down. Two figures that Brian recognized came stalking out of the smoke.

One of them was from the news. The blue-black furred werewolf that was easily his equal or better in size, his yellow eyes blazing. This was the same one that Brian remembered seeing being arrested two weeks ago.

The other, was a figure that made Brian's blood boil as he felt rage begin to burn.

Stepping out of the smoke and flame was a gigantic figure, broad in body, its blood red fur blending in with the carnage as his red eyes lit up with a savage joy. Dressed in similar combat gear, Rakinos stepped into the ruins of the foyer.

"Hello, Brian." He growled, a dark storm of a cold smile crossing over his muzzle.

Brian's hearing was still partially out and Rakinos and his words were distorted, echoing in a strange way as he fought to get to his feet and finally he did, standing, his clothes shredded from the blast, the silver chain and ring on his neck glistening in the burning halls.

"What the hell do you want?" Brian snarled at him, his fangs bared, his hands clenched into fists. He could feel his temper rising faster and struggled to keep it in check. He did not need to turn into that thing right now.

"You and Mullen, wherever he's currently cowering at." Rakinos told him bluntly as he directed his men to spread out. "And, I thought you'd like to see the fruits of my labor which, I honestly have to give you credit for. Without you, none of them would have been possible."

Rakinos motioned with his hand and a moment later Brian felt his heart hammer harder than it ever had. A freezing fear and terror began to flood his system as his ears flattened against his head and his tail unconsciously went between his legs, his eyes growing wide and the shadow monster from his dreams stepped into view.

It came from behind Rakinos, its fur the color of brown grave dirt, hulking with muscle and raw power. It towered over the seven-foot Rakinos and Brian's brain disconnectedly told him it was at least eight feet high. The head was like a wolf, too much like his own, but its eyes had no humanity in them. They were strange. One was blue, the other was yellow. Both were ringed with red. There was no soul there, nothing but rage and hate. A thick tail lashed behind it and its seven-inch black claws clicked like a spider's mandibles.

Its thickly furred body was naked from the waist up and from the waist down was clothed in some kind of high-tech fabric plate armor. On its right wrist some kind of high-tech bracelet or gauntlet that was grafted to its arm and from this gauntlet, Brian saw a glowing blue fluid being pumped into the creatures system.

It was then that Brian recognized the dead stare, the raw rage. The fluid was the drug that man in the hospital had been under. Raven's words came to haunt him.

A hyper stimulant with hypnotic qualities...

She and Molly were right in the meeting after all.

"You see," Rakinos told him as three more of the hulking monsters stalked into the room like mythological beasts, their heads nearly touching the ceiling.

"They wouldn't have been possible without your DNA. So, thank you, Mr. Mac-Gregor. Now, if you'd be so kind, I have need of you. You and Mr. Mullen will come with me or I will kill everyone in this house and burn it to the ground and I'll pin your eyelids open to make you watch. Your answer?"

Out of the corner of his eye, Brian saw Max crouched next to the thick banister, just out of sight and upstairs, he saw Molly come over the edge of the upper railing and saw metallic glint in her hands. He knew what that was. Brian didn't see Draco and that worried him. Next to him Ash was tensed, looking from each monster to each soldier, unsure of what to do. Two faces peeked out from behind Max; Jackson with a nasty scrape and blood leaking all over his face but otherwise unharmed and Raven, still in her human form, her cheek cut and bleeding.

They locked eyes and Max nodded.

Brian turned to face Rakinos. Rakinos shook his head.

"In case you were thinking of some heroic last-ditch effort, I did go out of my way to make sure I did have a bargaining chip."

A moment later there was a terrible struggle, the sounds of fists hitting flesh and then Roy was dragged out, handcuffed with a bleeding eyebrow, his flannel shirt ripped half off of him. He looked like he had been beaten within an inch of his life, and he was putting up one hell of a fight. John thrust Roy at Rakinos who caught the house manager with ease and wrapped his large red furred hands around the smaller shifter's neck.

"Now....your answer, McGregor? I'm going to get what I want either way."

Roy struggled under Rakinos and fought hard, bucking and trying to get loose which made Rakinos only tighten his grip.

"Fuck him, laddie. To hell with em all. Don't worry about me! Get out of here! They are gonna use you—"

Rakinos snarled and squeezed tighter, cutting off Roy's words.

"Let him go," Max said, his voice growing dangerously dark as he stood up from the corner, stepping into the burning firelight and moving to Brian's side, his blue eyes flaring yellow with hate. A muscle stood out in his jaw and Brian could tell he was gritting his teeth.

Rakinos chuckled.

"There you are. Come out of your hole, again? You know, when you first started beating up petty thugs in the alleys, I never stopped to even consider you a threat. And now...you and I have a lot of catching up to do-"

Without warning a silver blur shot out of the darkness like a bullet and with it, came a primal roar of canine rage and human anger. The blur slammed into Rakinos, knocking his grip on Roy free, sending the bigger shifter crashing through a wall into the coat room in a spray of wood sheetrock and dust.

Gunfire exploded but it wasn't from the soldiers but rather from upstairs. Bright popping orange flowers of muzzle flashes lit up as Molly picked her shots, landing four rounds into soldiers, expertly targeting their weak spots in their armor at the necks and face.

Four shifters dropped dead to the ground and the already insane world completely lost any coherence.

"KILL THEM ALL!" Rakinos roared from his crash site. "BRING ME MACGREGOR AND MULLEN ALIVE!" As he got to his feet, he was met with Draco, blocking his way, his white shirt dangling open with bloody gashes across his chest, panting in rage, his eyes blazing yellow with rage. His fangs were bared in a deadly snarl.

Soldiers condensed towards him, leveling their rifles.

"NO!" Max roared and dove into the fray to protect his surrogate father.

Fists struck armor plating, bones cracked and Max turned into a blur of motion. Blood filled the air as hot rounds began to fly as the soldiers opened fire on the enraged vigilante.

Brian and Ash leaped in as well, each one picking out a soldier and lighting into him. One soldier had lined up a shot on the back of Max's head and Brian saw it, snapping out his hands, grabbing the werewolf in a two-handed grip, and yanked backwards, twisting him around. Without hesitating, Brian drove a hard right hook into his face, dropping the soldier to the ground.

Max, panting, looked up at him and nodded. "Thanks…"

They dove back into the fray.

Ash laid out two more of them with solid roundhouse punches, shattering their face shields.

Upstairs, Molly managed to drop two more before picking out John's hulking blue-black form. She lined up her shot and planted two rounds squarely in his right shoulder while he was distracted. Roaring in rage and pain, he whirled on her and bolted up the stairs after her.

Jackson and Raven still crouched behind the banister.

"Jackson! Get that security system back on. The backup generators should have kicked on!" Molly barked, ducking as bullets chewed into the wood around them.

Roars and screams filled the air.

Jackson turned to Raven, yelling to be head over the chaos.

"They had to disconnect it outside but they may not have gotten to the generators through the old tunnels! If I can get them working again, I can get the power back on and reboot the defense grid!" he yelled over the noise.

Raven nodded. "GO!"

With that she stood up and rounded the corner and began to run at the nearest dog soldier. It saw her and snarled as Rakinos motioned them into action. Transforming into her wolf form as she ran, Raven's eyes flared purple and she leaped, landing on top of the giant beast, going at the back of its head with her fists and claws, using her smaller size to her advantage.

The other three dog soldiers took after Jackson, dropping to all fours as they moved, smashing down the hallway and vanishing into the darkness, the strange blue and yellowed beast in the lead.

The fires from the explosion had begun to spread, and now the drapes had caught fire, the flames roaring with their own hellish life, screaming towards the ceiling and even then the support beams on the roof had already began to smoke as the room grew hotter and harder to see in. The mercenaries couldn't fire easily at their opponents at such close range and so the brawl had devolved into a melee.

As Max, Raven, Brian and Ash were occupied fighting off the soldiers, Draco and Rakinos stood face to face, with open flame between them.

"You will not take my family from me. I should have never trusted you." Draco snarled at him, baring his white fangs.

Rakinos wiped the blood from the corner of his mouth.

"Oh yes. I will take them all, one by one and you will die knowing that it's all your fault for trusting me in the first place. After all, what kind of idiot invites the leader of a terrorist group into their home?"

A dawning look of realization spread across Draco's face.

"Lupine Freedom...You're their leader. That's why you did all of this..."

Rakinos bowed his head. "Got it in one."

With a roar, Draco charged him, the muscles in his arms bunching up as landed a brutal solid blow upside Rakinos face. Draco heard his own knuckles crack.

Rakinos was sent backwards and he tasted blood in mouth, the familiar coppery metallic taste flooding his senses. With a grunt he rolled with the punch and when Draco came at him again, Rakinos caught Draco's fist in midair.

Surprised, Draco swung with his free hand and Rakinos lashed out with a vicious kick that caught the older werewolf straight in the chest, sending him flying backward through the wall into the parlor with a violent explosion of wood and plaster.

Draco slammed to the ground as debris flew. The painting of St. Christopher fell from the wall, ripping into two pieces as it came down, glass littering the ground where Draco had been thrown through a display case.

Rakinos ran at him, claws out, teeth bared and Draco rolled over onto his back, the glass digging into the flesh, cutting him with a thousand tiny swords. He saw the hulking red werewolf charging and as Rakinos leaped, Draco raised his legs and planted his feet squarely into Rakinos's chest and shoved. Hard.

With a cry of surprise, Rakinos was flung head over heels, smashing down hard enough to shatter the same chair he had sat in two weeks ago, splintering the wooden floor with the force of his impact.

Draco got to his feet and by the time he had, Rakinos was up again. He spat out the blood in his mouth and squared his shoulders.

When he looked at Draco, Draco finally saw the insanity in those red eyes and knew then that Rakinos was enjoying this. Draco snarled, baring his fangs. He would not let this madman take his family.

"So, you do have some fight in you after all, old man. Good." Rakinos snarled, his deep voice making Draco's skin crawl.

With a roar, both combatants closed the distance and smashed into each other and the death dance began again.

#####

Brian was fighting for his life.

There was nothing now but motion, reflex and instinct. His rational mind had been reduced to an adrenaline smothered afterthought, riding the edge of the red line between his sanity and body and that darker something within him. The gunfire and the roaring was echoing background noise. He ducked as a soldier swung a knife in the air in front of his face, the blade parting the fur on his muzzle and he drove his fist through the shifter's plastic faceplate, shattering it and the snout behind it in a bone crushing blow. He felt the hot blood gush over his hand and he kicked out, landing a booted blow on the thick body armor, sending the werewolf to the ground.

He heard Ash grunt and turning, he saw that a soldier had him up against the wall.

Brian dropped down and picked up the dropped knife the soldier had been using on him and with a cry launched it at the soldier holding Ash.

With a sickening wet slash, the knife buried itself up to the hilt in the soldier's upper back. Crying out in rage and surprise, the soldier's attention was off Ash and that was when Ash slammed his forehead into the soldier's face, cracking his helmet, and dropped an elbow into the werewolf's throat, crushing his trachea. The soldier dropped like a sack of potatoes.

Max ducked two swings at his head and rolled as another soldier opened fire. The bullets sprayed into the soldier in front of Max, shredding his body armor, killing him instantly.

"CHECK YOUR FIRE!" one of the men screamed as Max drove a spinning kick into the back of his head.

"Consider it checked." Max snarled as he jerked his head up to see Raven struggling on the back of the dog soldier.

She had drawn blood, and it ran in rivers down the things back as she went for its eyes.

She made a mistake and gave up a secure spot for leverage and in that instant the dog soldier snared her forearm.

"RAVEN!" Max roared as the hulking monster yanked her off of its back and threw her like a rock.

Raven's white furred body sailed through the air and smashed into the far wall hard enough to leave a crater. With a cry she dropped to the ground stunned and nearly unconscious as the world swam in her eyes.

The dog soldier poised itself above her and raised its claws for the kill.

####

Molly ducked around the corner, planting her back firmly behind a thick hallway arch, the broad old beam behind her giving her comfort as her heart hammered away in her chest. She knew that the man chasing her, John Carrey was a wanted terrorist and fugitive. As her red hair hung in her face, she knew what he was capable of. She mentally counted how many rounds she had left.

At least seven.

It was her last clip; though she did have one last weapon besides her side arm but using it meant she was going to die most likely.

She had lost her flashlight in the melee and was now literally nearly blind in the dark halls of the cavernous manor house. Somewhere down the hall where she had just come from, she heard John's heavy foot falls ascend the stairs and enter the hallway.

"You know I'm going to kill you. Give up and I'll make it easy." He snarled, his voice trembling with inhuman rage.

Molly could hear his heavy breathing, could almost smell the musty scent of his unwashed fur.

Slowing her breathing she calmed herself, going back to her days at the academy; this asshole wasn't going to scare her and if he was going to kill her, she was going to give him hell the whole time he was at it.

Peeking around the corner, she saw his blue-black hulking from stalking the hallways and as he turned, she caught a glimpse of his blazing yellow eyes like cigarette embers in the dark. She lined up her shot at the back of his shoulders, and then moved her aim lower, aiming for his left elbow. It was the only one she could clearly make out in the moonlight of the windows.

She exhaled her breath and stabilized the glowing dot on the front blade of her pistol sight and squeezed the trigger.

The silver and black HK USP 9's slide bucked and a blossom of fire appeared at the end of its muzzle along with a deafening *BOOM*.

The round slammed home, hitting high, her aim off due to the darkness, biting into John's undefended tricep, cracking bone and tearing through tissue, sending up a spray of blood.

With a roar of agony and surprise he cradled his arm, looking down at it in shock, amazed she had been able to hit him in the darkness. Growling in pain, he

Anthony Milhorn

straightened his arm, gritting his teeth against the agony; he knew it would take days to heal that damage. It enraged him further, and as he turned, he saw her there, peeking out from around a corner like a human rat, the smoking gun in her hands.

She was going to die slowly, he decided. No human hurt him and lived. The ghostly scent of his own burning flesh from that brand years ago haunted him.

He roared and charged at her, planning to use his teeth, his claws, his bare hands, whatever he hand to take her down, wounded arm or not.

Molly rounded the corner and stood facing him and raised her gun, leveling herself into the Weaver Stance and opened fire, discharging round after round after round.

In the dark most of them missed their mark and some of them hit home, smacking into John's chest and stomach and thick legs with wet splotches, making him stumble.

He was almost on her when the slide locked back and the sound of an empty chamber echoed loudly in her ears.

Not wasting a second, Molly cast aside the gun and reached into her loose pant suit jacket and yanked a silver tube from her belt and flicked it. It expanded into a nightstick like device and with a flick of a switch, lightning curled around its edges with a sharp whine.

As John fell upon her, she swung it for all she was worth.

#####

"FUCK FUCK FUCK!" Jackson yelled to himself as he pounded down the halls, grateful he could see in the dark, stumbling around a corner. He heard the massive rapid footfalls behind him and he knew that those monsters would be upon him at any moment. He could almost feel their fangs at the back of his throat, feel their claws ripping into his tender flesh.

Sliding around a corner on a rug, he took the basement stairs two at a time and finally arrived at the server room and knew the fuse box and generator room was just through the server room itself. The server room door had slid open automatically once the power was lost but the fuse room and generator area were sealed off by a heavy steel door with a lock that was totally manual. If he could get there, he could seal the dog soldiers out and secure the generator room. From there he could easily take the crawl space back up to the main foyer.

A roar behind him and the sound of splintered wood put more speed into his steps and he brushed the blood out of his eyes as he passed through the server room door, squeezing through the tight space.

Behind him the dog soldiers crashed through the stairway, leaping it entirely and a moment later, he heard the cracking sound of glass and steel as they tried to shove their way into the server room. Looking back, Jackson saw them there, a pair of shimmering blue and yellow eyes in the lead of the pack. One of them reached up and drove its claws into the steel door frame shredding it like paper and it shoved, breaking the door totally out of its frame and smashing through the rest of the glass, leaving a now gaping hole straight into the server room.

"SHIT!" Jackson yelped as he saw the thick steel door that led to the generator room. It was open and with the last surge of adrenaline he leaped through it and turned immediately to slam it shut.

It wouldn't budge.

"No!! FUCK!" he bellowed to himself in shock.

He shoved harder. The dog soldiers took a moment, slowing down a fraction as they sniffed him out and they saw him a moment later as the lead with the mismatched eyes stood to tower on his hind legs and bared it fangs at him unleashing a roar that shook the room.

Jackson shoved and pushed. The door wouldn't move.

He wasn't going to die here, not this way. Not this night.

The dog soldiers charged at him and with scream of defiance, Jackson put every ounce of his strength into it and the door swung shut and falling to his knees, he slammed the heavy lock home.

The dog soldiers slammed into with a snarl of frustration.

They hit it hard, shaking the entire thing, rattling the world it seemed but for now, they were stuck out there and he was in here.

He quickly surveyed the room and felt his heart drop.

His blood ran cold at what he saw there.

The soldiers had already been in here. How he didn't know. They must have come down in here before they blew the wall upstairs. He saw his answer a moment later. There was a huge hole in the far wall, cut with plasma cutters. Quiet and deadly. Somehow they had found an old tunnel from the previous foundation but that wasn't what now held his attention.

What held his attention now, was far worse.

The entire room, generators included, were lined with plastic bricks made up of a grey white paste. Wires stuck out of the blocks and each block was glowing with a red and a green light. A wireless transmitter ran from several of them.

C4.

Jackson realized that no matter what happened upstairs, Rakinos was going to blow them all sky high. There was no way he could restart the security system or the generator without killing them all.

The dog soldiers hammered on the door and it groaned, bending in the middle as reinforced claws scraped down the metal biting into it.

The only thing to do was to get out and escape. He had to warn the others.

Frantically, Jackson hurled aside the shelving that hid the false wall. This house was built on the foundations of an earlier property and that property had been a part of the Underground Railroad and so, the house's foundations had tunnels running all through them. Rather than brick them up, Draco had Jackson use them to run all the fiber optics and cables and now, he could use this one to get back up the main foyer, just like the psychos upstairs used it to lay a trap. As he dove into the cramped space and began to half climb half crawl, he hoped he wasn't too late.

####

Rakinos had slowly gained the upper hand as Draco had begun to tire. True, Draco was about the same size and weight as Rakinos but Rakinos had one thing on him that the old man never could have.

Rakinos lacked any sense of honor or empathy and that worked tremendously in his advantage but unlike Draco, Rakinos wasn't going to hesitate to kill. Draco didn't have the rage that fueled Rakinos.

The parlor library was a mess. Furniture lay broken, display cases obliterated and the antique pieces lay in ruin. The searing flames had now reached the parlor walls and were beginning to lick at the floors and ceilings hungrily.

Draco swung at Rakinos hard and nearly made contact but Rakinos moved just the right way and Draco missed.

Deciding this game was over, Rakinos stopped toying with the old man and drove a solid fist into the side of Draco's head. He heard bone crack and blood ran from Draco's ear.

"There's a difference between you..." Rakinos snarled driving a second blow into Draco's head this time from the right.

"...And me!" Rakinos barked sending a knee into Draco's chest. Draco tried to recover but Rakinos gave no quarter and drove him towards the windows that looked out into the front yard.

Draco tried to charge him but Rakinos side stepped him and drove an elbow into Draco's neck. With a yelp of pain and exhaustion, Draco crashed to the ground on his belly. Rakinos stepped over him, straddling him before grabbing him by the back of his neck, hauling Draco to his feet, spinning him around to face him, dragging him to his feet.

"The difference is I'm willing to do whatever I need to get what I want and you're in my way." Rakinos snarled harshly into the older werewolf's face.

Rakinos let go of Draco and drove three blows into Draco's chest and stomach, cracking four ribs with wet meaty snaps and inside, Draco felt something rupture from the sheer force as he stumbled to stay on his feet. He hadn't fought like this in many years and he knew that this fight was already lost. As thoughts of his family shot through his mind, Rakinos roundhouse kicked Draco with all of his strength.

The blow impacted square in the center Draco's broad chest with the sound of a hammer striking a thick side of steak and Draco went flying backward, smashing through the floor to ceiling window. Distantly, Draco heard the splintering panes and the ear-splitting shriek of tortured glass as it exploded all around him. The world spun crazily and a moment later, he hit the hard, unforgiving ground, driving all the remaining fight out of him as he hit and rolled to a stop twenty feet from the house itself, laying in a pool of blood and shattered shards of glass.

Rakinos leaped out of the broken window and came down with a crash, shaking the earth. He stooped and picked up a nasty curving piece of glass from beside

Draco and he knelt down low, looking Draco in the eyes, flipping him onto his back so he could look Draco in the eyes as he spoke, his voice low and rumbling with hate.

"You know, we could have worked together. We could have taken over. Had it all but you had to grow a conscience all those years ago. Let me fix that for you."

Rakinos drove the glass blade into Draco's right kidney, twisting it, breaking it off cleanly deep inside the old werewolf's body. Draco howled in pain but the fight was thoroughly out of him. Behind them, the manor had begun to burn properly, casting wild shadows upon the peaceful grounds and the moon hovered over everything, slowly drowning to ever thickening smoke.

Rakinos leaned in to Draco's good ear and whispered to him.

"I know you won't die from that right away. You'll eventually keel over from it. Your immune system can't repair itself fast enough with the damage I've done and that means you're going to live long enough to see me take everything from you and I want you to know, you invited me here. All of this lays upon you."

With a savage kick, Rakinos drove his foot into the side of Draco's head and Draco's body went limp with unconsciousness as Rakinos stalked back towards the house.

#####

Molly ducked a claw swipe at her head and drove her electric baton deep into John's side, slamming it home with a crunch of metal on flesh.

Sparks flew violently, lighting up the hallway. The smell of burnt hair and skin flooded her nostrils as he howled in rage and pain, stumbling back from her.

Pressing her opening she swung it again, hitting him in the thighs, the wrist, the stomach, anywhere she could reach, each blow landing with the sharp metallic crack and the explosive sizzle of artificial lightning. Blue energy raced up and down the baton and John was forced backward, the powerful electrical shocks overwhelming his nervous system.

She drove him down the hall and finally had his back to one of the big windows that led to a straight drop to the ground below. John ducked her next swing and she missed his head, smashing out the window itself. She nearly lost her balance and went out of it but managed to right herself before it was too late.

John was upon her and she found she couldn't breathe because he managed to catch her in a stranglehold. Growling savagely, he lifted, picking her up off the ground. Molly could hear the bones in her neck creak and protest as her heart demanded more oxygen that simply would not come.

"A human branded me once; I swore I'd never let a human hurt me again." He bared his fangs at her and she knew that if she didn't do something she was going to die so he pulled the oldest trick in the book.

She rammed her feet, heels first, into his crotch with a satisfying thud.

Werewolf or not, he was still a man and it worked. He dropped her hard to the ground as he went down to his knees, howling in agony, cupping himself. Molly landed hard on her knees, gasping for breath. She saw John moving towards her and didn't hesitate. Climbing to her feet, she recovered the electric baton she had dropped when he snared her and raised it back like a baseball bat.

John looked up at her, his face a mix of rage and blind hate, his yellow eyes flaring as he opened his jaws to dive at her and rip her throat out.

Molly swung the baton with every bit of strength she had, letting loose an adrenaline-fueled battle cry. The sparking baton whistled as it moved through the air and slammed into John's right eye socket, sending him reeling backwards, blinded and unstable. Molly kicked out with her left foot, catching him in the chest and she watched the surprise and shock come over his face as he fell backward, out of the shattered window.

For a moment he pin wheeled there, and then gravity snared him and with a vicious roar of defeat, John went out of the window and spiraled down to the ground below where he impacted with a deep *WHUMP.*

Molly looked over the edge and saw his crumpled body lying there and blew a strand of hair out of her face.

Panting she turned and made for the foyer. There was still a battle to be fought.

#####

The normal werewolf soldiers lay defeated, most of them dead or severely injured. Two of them were stirring but barely.

Raven blinked, looked up and saw the black clawed monster swinging for her head.

She was going to die.

A moment later a black streak shot of the corner of her eye and took the blow for her.

It was Brian.

He had jumped between the dog soldier and Raven and she felt the hot spray of his blood as the things cruel claws raked him from the shoulder down to his hip as he tackled it away from her.

"BRIAN!" Max yelled.

Brian's tackle pushed the dog soldier backward but not far and it kicked him aside like street trash. He tucked and rolled coming up to his feet, his face a mask of pain and anger and yes, fear, his green eyes wide.

Max was there, swinging a piece of heavy wood from the stairs that he had ripped loose. The dog soldier whirled on him and the wood smashed it across the face, exploding into splinters.

With a snarl, it stumbled backward, blood running from its eyes, nose and face as the splinters stabbed home.

It backhanded Max, sending him flying back into the stairs. He landed hard, the wind driven from him as the dog soldier advanced on him.

"Oi, you overgrown beast!"

The dog soldier roared in pain as Roy appeared and rammed a thick gardening scythe into the thing's ribcage, shoving it home with such force it was buried up to the hilt.

The dog soldier snarled in an even deeper rage and whirled on Roy. Roy swung at it with a piece of burning debris and missed as the dog soldier snapped its clawed hands out and picked him up, snatching him right off his feet.

It all happened so fast that no one could have done anything.

The dog soldier yanked Roy close, snarling in his face, black fangs dripping with saliva.

"Go to hell." Roy spat in its face.

With an ungodly roar, the dog soldier reared back and threw Roy across the room straight into a pile of burning debris. Roy never even had time to yell as a piece of searing support beam that had been knocked loose erupted from his chest, impaling him. His body lay still, his eyes unseeing as the warm yellow light in them faded.

"NO!" Max snarled and threw himself at the dog soldier. Brian joined him and together they fought the creature with everything that had, each one taking horrendous blows from it. Its claws ripped open their chests, drawing blood.

Ash, blood streaking his snout, looked into the parlor where Draco had been and panic filled him. His brother wasn't there. There room was soaked in blood and fire was rapidly consuming it.

Hoping that Max and the others could handle the monstrosity, Ash turned to find Draco, throwing open the huge door that led outside, searing his hands in the process from the hot metal of the door knob. Cursing, he pressed on and there, he saw his brother, lying unmoving in the yard, a dark pool beneath him.

His eyes went wide and there, coming towards the house, was the red furred hulking demon himself, Rakinos.

With an angry cry, Ash drove himself at Rakinos, fully intending to rip his head off his ugly shoulders.

Rakinos backhanded him across the temple, sending Ash flying a good thirty feet crashing into the underbrush at the bottom of one of the statues and he didn't get back up. Rakinos continued on towards the burning manor, his own temper very much over the red line.

This had gone on long enough.

#####

Raven had seen a weak spot. The wrist gauntlet. It regulated the flow of the stabilizing chemicals into the creature. If they could take it out, then they could likely drive the creature itself insane enough to bring it down. She was about to shout at Max and Brian who were losing to it badly when a hulking shadow fell over her.

She tried to roll out of the way when it reached down and grabbed her. She felt herself be lifted up by the throat and she couldn't scream, couldn't warn them as Rakinos entered the house again, dragging her along with him.

Rakinos held Raven tightly, ignoring her kicks and punches. He looked up and saw Molly appear at the top of the staircase, electric baton in hand and saw that John had not been successful. A part of Rakinos would miss him. Then again, if he hadn't been up to the task...An acceptable loss.

He squeezed Raven's neck harder.

"STOP!" he bellowed.

The dog soldier threw both Max and Brian aside, both of them badly beaten and bloody. They landed in a heap, panting for breath.

The dog soldier moved as if to go after them when Rakinos tapped a control on his belt and with an electric sizzle, the dog soldier stopped in its tracks and growled angrily but did not move. He wondered where the other three were but in the moment, he didn't have time to think about it. If they were as savage as he thought, then that may explain the smaller werewolf...what was his name? Jackson. Yes. That might explain his absence. He wondered if the dog soldiers were cannibalistic. Whatever got the job done. He quickly refocused on the task at hand.

"If anyone moves, she dies!" Rakinos roared and squeezed Raven's neck harder. He heard her bones crack.

Good.

"Don't...listen...to..." she tried to speak and Rakinos squeezed off her air way entirely shutting her up. He squeezed tighter for a good ten seconds until she nearly blacked out and then let go again. She gasped in ragged breaths, her neck burning. Rakinos continued, the flames crackling around them.

"I want MacGregor and Mullen to surrender. They come with me. The rest of you can live. Refuse and she dies right here. Then I'll take you both anyway and kill each one of your surviving your friends in front you, slowly, one by one."

He paused for effect.

"CHOOSE NOW!" he bellowed, his eyes flaring scarlet, his chest heaving, fur gleaming in the firelight as the manor had finally began to burn in earnest.

Max and Brian looked at each other. Max shook his head as he saw a look come over Brian's face.

They debated silently and finally, both of them stood up together.

"Don't hurt anyone else. We'll go with you." Brian said putting his hands up, panting, his body aching in a thousand places, blood soaking his fur.

Rakinos smiled. "Good. Maybe you aren't entirely stupid after all."

Two of the surviving normal werewolf soldiers who had gotten to their feet not so dead after all rushed forward, rifles leveled at Brian and Max's head. One of them lowered his gun and reached around his back. When his hands came back around, Brian saw Max stiffen.

In the soldiers hands were two sets of cuffs that looked like they could fit over the entire wrist, like a gauntlet. Max was restraining himself from lashing out as the soldier snapped the cuffs shut around Brian's wrist and then around his own. A moment later, a red light winked on.

Brian moved his arms and suddenly felt searing pain as 10,000 volts exploded into his nervous system, sending him to his knees.

Max snarled, his eyes blazing as he pinned Rakinos with his stare.

Shock cuffs. The bastard was using Madison Genetics shock cuffs.

The electrical impulses were designed specifically to target the hypersensitive nervous system of werewolves and disrupt it, like a taser on steroids.

Once Brian stopped struggling, the shocks dissipated.

"Get them to the transport truck. Keep them separate." Rakinos barked.

With a disgusted look, he hurled Raven across the room. She landed hard, skidding across the broken wood, rolling to a stop just before the staircase.

Molly came down the stairs, her neck badly bruised, and knelt beside her, helping her to her feet. Raven's white fur was stained red in places and Molly knew some of that was her own blood.

She cast a sorrowful glance that became silent rage at Roy's still body and a terrible realization began to eat at her. She looked around quickly as panic threatened to take over.

Draco. Where was he? Where was Ash? Where were the other three creatures? Where's Jackson?!

She said nothing as she pulled Raven into a sitting position. Raven groaned but she was alive.

As the soldiers led Brian and Max grudgingly out, Rakinos and the dog soldier followed them. Molly watched them go and about half way out into the driveway, Rakinos motioned to one of the soldiers who turned around and pulled something round from his belt and threw it.

Molly recognized it and threw herself over Raven as the grenade landed with a clink of metal on wood and a second later it erupted into a titanic fireball. The explosion ripped apart foyer, bringing the roof down, blocking off any escape out of the foyer or out of the house itself, trapping them all inside a burning death trap.

Molly's ears were ringing as she looked up and saw the tomb they were now in. Even if Rakinos didn't kill them, unless they could escape they were would die burning alive or from smoke inhalation.

Coughing, she tried to drag Raven, who was having a hard time standing, off the stairs and towards the one hall that wasn't blocked. As she did, she caught motion at the corner of her eye near the floor and looked down.

A chunk of the wall had cracked open in a perfect square and there, behind it, was Jackson. He was covered in dirt and blood and grit and when he looked up and saw Molly and Raven, he sighed in relief.

"Thank god! They've rigged the whole house to blow. We've gotta get out of here! NOW!" he yelled.

"We can't! Rakinos blew the foyer shut!" Molly looked down the hallway she thought was clear and felt her heart drop. The fire had collapsed it. "The other hallway is collapsed!"

"Come on! These old tunnels go under the lake. We can get out at the exit down there but we gotta move now!"

"Help me!" Molly barked and Jackson reached up and grabbed Raven's legs and the two of them moved as fast they could and got her into the tunnel. Molly herself went in next and pulled the false wall shut behind her.

Out in the yard, Max struggled against his captors, throwing himself at Rakinos only to have the cuffs stun him into near unconsciousness. He roared with rage and pain but was helpless to watch as his second home burned the ground with his family inside it all over again.

Brian lunged at Rakinos as well, regardless of the cuffs. Rakinos cold cocked him, sending him sprawling. Max started forward again but Rakinos grabbed him by the throat and personally dragged him to the transport truck that had been parked just out of sight, throwing the titanium door open wide. With a heave, Rakinos threw Max into the tiny transport cell and slammed the door in his face, sealing it with a magnetic lock and bolt.

"Mr. MacGregor you are going to help me reshape the world in a new image." Rakinos told Brian as the soldiers yanked Brian up and threw him bodily into the back of the vehicle, sealing the door behind him.

"My image." Rakinos told him coldly. He motioned for the two surviving soldiers and dog soldier to pack it up and they did. A moment later, the truck was idling, waiting on Rakinos to leave. A thought struck him. He had one final promise to keep. He moved quickly back to where he had left Draco.

Rakinos stood over Draco's limp body and for a moment, he thought the old man had died. Then he satisfyingly saw that Draco was still breathing. Barely but enough. He reached down and grabbed Draco by the scruff of the neck and began to drag him back to the circular driveway. Draco didn't fight back, his body weakened from blood loss and shock.

Once he was in the driveway, Rakinos roughly picked up Draco and slammed him down hard, yanking him up into a sitting position, facing the house, leaning against the heavy stone of the center fountain. Draco opened his blood shot eyes and frowned at Rakinos, his vision unfocused at first and then realizing who was holding him up, Draco tried to put up one final fight. Rakinos easily forced him back down.

"No no no... you just need sit right there." Rakinos snarled, holding him in place as he reached around to the back of his belt and brought out a small box about the size of a cellular phone. It had a flip switch cover and beneath that switch was a red glowing button. A small antenna made of rubber came off the other end. Flipping up the switch cover, Rakinos showed the box to Draco whose eyes went wide with fear and panic as he looked from the box to the burning house, knowing that his family, what was left of it, to his knowledge, Max, Brian, Raven, Molly, Jackson, Ash...all of them, were still in there.

He struggled to form words. "Please...don't...do...this..."

In the transport truck, despite the electric shocks, Brian and Max had managed to pull themselves up and through the transport cell's thick barred tiny windows, they saw the manor engulfed and saw Rakinos kneeling next to a broken, bloody, barely moving form with something in his hand.

As the moon light and smoke cleared, Max saw that it was Draco.

He felt something leap in his throat. Something painful as an old wound ripped open all over again. No. This was not happening again. It couldn't happen again.

Max felt his heart hammer and his blood run cold. His ears lay flat against his skull and he didn't hear it but he was making a whining noise, a whimper as he struggled against the electric shocks on his wrists to say something, anything, to do anything, to get out there.

Rakinos knelt next to Draco and leaned in close.

"I want you in your dying moments to remember these words and know they are true, as true as that fire there. If it wasn't for you, I would have never known about Brian. All of this.... all of this death....is your fault. You murdered your own family with your heart and, there's only one thing left to do about that..."

Draco struggled against Rakinos but his body was too weak. Rakinos simply held him down with one hand and held the detonator up with the other. Draco looked at Rakinos and for the first time in his life he begged through a mouthful of blood.

"Nooo..." Draco tried to speak, shaking. "It...doesn't...have to ...be this...way..."

Rakinos considered that and he felt eyes on him and he looked up slowly, turning his head towards the transport truck. He saw Max Mullen there and Brian, both of them yelling at him, incoherent from the pain of their shock cuffs, mixed growls and yelps of pain and agony.

Rakinos fixed his red eyes on Max in particular with a cold stare full of a strange singular hatred, meeting the younger shifter's blue eyes. They had lost their yellow fire from the pain of the cuffs. Now, all Rakinos saw in them was fear, a familiar fear, a fear from twenty-two years ago. In that moment, Rakinos knew the DNA tests were right.

Standing up and walking back to the transport truck, its red tail lights flaring, its engine roaring, Rakinos left Draco to watch his life burn. As he got up to the truck, he stopped at the cages and looked up into Max's pleading eyes, so full of fear and pain and hate all at once. He heard Max's mixed yelps of pain and whimpers, pleading with Rakinos. Rakinos thought he could get used to that. He also knew that the remaining three dog soldiers were will trapped inside the house. They were expendable and the distance between himself and the house was sufficient.

As he looked into Max's eyes again, the house burning behind them, Rakinos leaned in where Max alone could hear him and finished his sentence with a deadly certain finality.

"Yes. It does."

Rakinos depressed the detonator stud.

With a click and a beep, Max's nightmares became a reality all over again as Forest Glen erupted into a fireball that consumed the entire house.

Max never heard himself scream but he did. It was a single word.

"NO!!!!!!!!!!!!!!!!!!!"

The earth itself shook and night became day. The ancient stone walls and windows blew out, years of family history went up in an inferno as the shock wave screamed out into the night rattling the truck itself. Rakinos leaped into the truck and it sped away, bouncing down the rutted road.

Max heard himself screaming in rage and horror, unable to do anything as his only family was torn away from him again. He rammed himself into the side of the cage over and over, nearly breaking his shoulder, ignoring the spark from his cuffs, smelling his own burning crisping fur, his teeth gnashing, eyes wild.

It did no good.

The fireball faded into a raging tower of fire and jet-black smoke as the last remnants of Forest Glen collapsed into the burning crackling crater that had once been a place of warmth, light and hope.

At last Max collapsed to the floor of the truck, stunned into submission from the cuffs. He was crying from raw rage and pain, his body unable to fight off the electricity any longer as the cuffs stunned him into unconsciousness and merciful blackness over took him. Even then, he whimpered in his nightmares.

Brian watched the manor burn, watched the last of the old home collapse, and felt his whole world go dark and empty. He didn't fight the cuffs.

He didn't have the strength anymore.

He simply collapsed onto his behind and felt his heart utterly break as he could hear Max screaming as tears of agony and loss poured from the man he loved before he passed out and there was nothing he could do to comfort him. No words, nothing could ever heal the damage that was just done to him. He couldn't even reach him or touch him. He was isolated, alone with his suffering.

Brian felt numbness take him and as the truck bounced, taking him away from everything he had come to know, taking him away towards an unknown fate, he laid his head back against the truck wall and let the tears flow silently down his black furred face and knew it was over.

Rakinos had won.

He's taken everything.....everyone... and it's all because of me. All of this is my fault....

This echoed in Brian's thoughts for miles until he too finally passed out from exhaustion and blood loss and when unconsciousness came for him, he welcomed its death-like embrace and surrendered to the dark where there was no more pain.

Made in the USA
Middletown, DE
02 April 2025